PLAYING HURT

PLAYING HURT

GERALD L. NARDELLA

ARPress
45 Dan Road Suite 5
Canton MA 02021
Hotline: 1(888) 821-0229
Fax: 1(508) 545-7580

Ordering Information:

Quantity sales. Special discounts are available on quantity purchases by corporations, associations, and others. For details, contact the publisher at the address above.

Printed in the United States of America.

ISBN-13:   Softcover   979-8-89330-265-3

                  eBook   979-8-89330-264-6

Library of Congress Control Number: 2024901485

PLAYING HURT
BY GERALD L. NARDELLA

"Whenever she came near, he hated the role he had to play, pretending she didn't matter anymore."

Set in the 1960s, this novel features high school students Brian Wheeler and Deanie Cummings who are madly in love with each other. But recently, Deanie has been quite distant towards Brian after their first time having sex. To make matters worse, Deanie's ex-boyfriend, Bill Slater, is back in town. The last time they saw each other, things did not go so well. Since his return, he has been pursuing Deanie, even though he knows she has moved on with someone else. One day, Bill forces her to have sex with him. Deanie is in shock and doesn't tell anybody about it. Brian senses that something must have happened between Deanie and Bill, so he breaks up with her. This break-up affects her deeply, and she spirals out of control with consequences that will affect her future.

Nardella dives into the characters' emotions and psychological state. For instance, she shows how Deanie is conflicted by her sexual activities. She feels guilty and remorseful, which leads to tears after she has sex with Brian. From there, she wants to take things slowly. She had planned to remain a virgin until marriage. However, as a result of her actions with Brian, she feels like she has broken a promise to herself. Nardella uses a confessional technique popular in narratives by having her protagonist reveal these thoughts to her friend, Karen. Deanie then establishes a sharp contrast between Karen and herself. Karen was able to stand firm and refuse to sleep with her boyfriend, while Deanie feels that she gave up too easily. Deanie's intense struggle with her thoughts and emotions helps make her relatable to the reader. Many will likely appreciate this book because the characters express their emotions with honesty.

- US Review of Books

The following excerpt is from an official review by <u>Onlinebookclub.org</u>

Playing Hurt by Gerald L. Nardella is a relatable and starkly realistic narrative about high school drama and social pressures in the 1960s. It follows two teenagers Brian and Deanie, as they navigate the trials of their senior year. There is a heavy emphasis on sex, as it pertains to adolescents who are just starting to understand the subject. The most remarkable thing about *Playing Hurt*, though, is its down-to-earth depiction of the conflicting pressures in both boys' and girls' lives regarding sex and relationships.

The writing style of *Playing Hurt* is straightforward and clean, with enough description to give readers a sense of the characters and environment, but not enough to bog down the story. It's a quick read, and is shockingly compelling for its length.

Playing Hurt is for those who enjoy character-driven narratives that focus on these themes, and can be of particular interest to anyone looking to better understand the confusion towards sexuality felt by adolescents. It's a gem of story, and remarkably moving.

— By ViziVoir

Chapter One

A steady stream of blood continued to drip from Brian West's hand as he stepped in close behind Jack Wheeler, the center. Four plays earlier, someone's cleat ripped open his left index finger, and pressing it against his thigh pad hadn't stopped the bleeding. Now, each time he positioned his hands under Wheeler for the snap, more and more blood transferred onto Wheeler's white football pants, leaving noticeable red streaks on his inner thighs and crotch, offering an easy opportunity for ridicule.

"What's the matter, Wheeler?" Dan Buckley, the right tackle, had asked in the last huddle. "Forget your tampon this morning?"

Wheeler bent over to look between his legs. "Damn it, West, go get your hand bandaged."

Afraid the coach might pull him from the game, Brian shook the blood from his finger and hurried and called another play. There were only two minutes left in this final game of the season, and there was a chance the Park County High Rangers could actually pull off a win—the first win of the 1960 season. It had been a humiliating year. The prior week's loss to Missoula was 52 to 0. Now to the amazement of everyone, Livingston was down by only two points against their biggest rival, the Bozeman Hawks. The offense had driven the ball down to the Hawks' thirty-yard line and was poised to get another touchdown.

The wooden bleachers were full, with Livingston fans all crowded together on the east side of the field. The enthusiastic Bozeman fans who had traveled over the winding twenty-six-mile pass rooted boisterously on the opposite side.

It was a chilly October night, and Brian's breath clouded out in front of him as he barked out the calls. He glanced up and down the line at the steaming red-and-black jerseys of the Hawks. The air was filled with muddled voices, laughter, and shrill whistles, while the rhythmic beat of the bass drum boomed out and across the field, fading away quickly into the darkness. To the south, a half-moon was rising from behind the jagged mountain ridges. A brisk canyon breeze swayed the tops of cottonwoods, dislodging drying leaves and swirling them into bunches high in the overhead lights of the field.

At the snap, Brian handed off to Dick Dana, the right halfback and Brian's best friend. The play was to run over the right tackle, but before Dick could reach the line of scrimmage, the Hawks' middle linebacker crashed through, clobbering Dick for a four-yard loss.

"Nice fucking block, Buckley," Dick said, glaring up at Dan Buckley.

Buckley's thick face turned a deep shade of red. His two upper-front teeth had been broken off during a fistfight back in the eighth grade and as he bared his clinched teeth, the gold gaps glittered in the lights.

"Kiss my ass, Dana," Buckley bellowed. He made a lunge for Dana, but Ray Hudson, the left tackle, was quick to step between them.

By then, everyone in the huddle was arguing as to who was or wasn't doing their jobs. Brian called time out and hurried over to the sidelines. As he stood next to Coach LeClaire, the trainer hurried to wrap gauze and tape around his bleeding finger. Down the sidelines, he could see Deanie Cummings, grouped with the other two cheerleaders, in front of the school band. She looked beautiful in her purple-and-gold cheerleader's outfit, her long blonde hair bouncing against her shoulders and her skirt bobbing against her slender bare thighs. He hoped she would smile or wave, but it was obvious she was still angry and wouldn't make eye contact with him. It was disappointing that his mother wasn't in the stands to watch his final game, yet she seldom came to his games. She was working a double shift at the truck stop. "But I'll be thinking of you," she told him. The only other person there he cared about was his boss, Orlen Picard, who sat at the top of the bleachers with his friend Joe Parker, sharing and seemingly enjoying a bottle of something concealed in a brown paper sack. His grandfather on his mother's side used to come to his games. He was the one person who encouraged him to participate in sports.

"You're built like me," he said. "You're too damn short to play basketball, but you're muscular enough to play football and baseball."

He died of leukemia before Brian started high school, and Brian missed seeing him in the stands. Oddly, he often thought of his own father during games. He never knew him, but he'd seen pictures of him. The pictures were from a Park High annual his mother kept and a few snapshots. He looked no older than Brian now. He left town before Brian was born. His mother's family thought Brian looked much like his father, although Brian's hair was light like his mother's. His mother entered his father's last name, West, on his birth certificate. Brian never knew the reason he left, except perhaps he was just too young to care for a family.

"I haven't seen such chicken-shit blocking since grade school," Coach LeClaire blurted out, rubbing his thick cheeks and nervously shuffling his feet.

Brian could smell whiskey on his breath.

"It's their middle linebacker," Brian said. "He's been a real pain in the ass."

The coach noticed Brian's finger. "How'd that happen?"

"Somebody stepped on it," Brian said.

"Well, there's nobody else who can do this, West. You'll just have to play hurt."

"I'll be all right, Coach."

"You go out there and tell Buckley and the rest of the line to kick some ass."

The trainer finished with Brian's finger, but before Brian could turn and run back out on the field, the coach grabbed him by the shoulder pad.

"Run a screen pass," the coach said. "That'll fix him."

Brian looked downfield once more at Deanie. Dick had told him he was getting too serious over her. Perhaps he was. He couldn't keep his mind off her and what happened the night before.

Back at the huddle, the wrangling hadn't diminished. Buckley was threatening to beat up everyone. Better known for his fighting abilities than his athletic skills, he weighed nearly two hundred forty pounds. He and his sidekick, Ray Hudson, were at the top of the Park High food chain. One assistant coach referred to them as his favorite street athletes.

Listening to the bickering, Brian glanced around the huddle at all the angry faces. He had grown up with most of them, sharing countless locker rooms and benches with them. With the exception of Dick, none of them ever became close friends. Like Buckley and Hudson, most of them were street fighters. Buckley was already on probation for beating up a thirty-five year old man earlier in the year. The man ended up in the hospital after Buckley kicked him in the head. It took a great deal of political persuasion from his dad to get the school to let him play football.

"Okay, listen up, guys!" Brian shouted to get everyone's attention. "We've actually got a chance to win this thing."

When Brian relayed what Coach LeClaire said about getting tough, Buckley blurted out mockingly, "Kick ass? I'll show you some ass kicking."

Finally, the grumbling lessened, and Brian called a play. The screen pass worked as the whole Hawks' line came rushing at Brian, decoying backward. Leaping as high as he could, he threw the ball off in the direction of Dick on the right flank, just before getting slammed to the ground. He didn't see the reception, but he heard the cheers. Dick made it to the fifteen-yard line but remained on the ground, clutching his leg and groaning. When Dan Buckley arrived downfield, he found the Hawks' middle linebacker straddling above Dana, cheering triumphantly.

Buckley casually walked up to the linebacker. Smiling, he said, "What's your problem, asshole?"

The linebacker was a few inches taller, but Buckley was clearly the bigger man.

"It was just a lucky catch," the linebacker said. "Your team is a bunch of losers. There is no way you are going to win this game."

Buckley didn't reply but grabbed for the linebacker's facemask. With one quick jerk of his left hand, Buckley popped loose the chinstrap, lifted up the helmet, and promptly smashed his fist into the linebacker's exposed face. Blood splattered across the striped shirt of the line judge. Pushing and shoving quickly followed, and the referee motioned that Buckley be ejected from the game. The trainer came out to look at Dick's leg and to help him up. Dick tried but couldn't put his full weight on his foot. He too had to leave the game.

After the penalty, the ball ended up on the thirty-yard line. There was less than a minute left in the game.

"Listen up," Brian ordered in the huddle. "If ever you guys remembered anything about blocking, now is the time to do it. For some of us, this is probably the last play of the last game we'll ever play. Let's go out winners."

Brian called a pass play with the backs and ends crisscrossing just at the goal line. The Hawks' middle linebacker was back in position, looking as determined as ever, but with dried blood smeared across his face. Dick was on the bench shouting encouragement. Buckley stood on the sidelines screaming obscenities.

Brian had a clear shot at his right end. He threw a perfect spiral, and all the receiver had to do was to catch the ball and step across the goal line. But disbelievingly, the ball deflected off his shoulder pads and ended up in the arms of the infamous Hawks' middle linebacker. With the ball tucked tightly in his arms, the linebacker raced across the field toward the sidelines. Once there, he turned up field, switching on his afterburners. It looked for sure that he would go all the way for a touchdown. The only mistake he made was picking the wrong sideline to run along: Dan Buckley's side. Buckley had the play timed perfectly. Just as the linebacker got even with the Rangers' bench, Buckley lunged out at him, smacking him just under his left ribcage, knocking him five yards sideways and leaving him sprawled out on the field. The ball popped loose, and Ray Hudson picked it up just as the gun sounded. There was a lot of shouting and whistle blowing, but Hudson ran the ball all the way to the end zone anyway.

Buckley was immediately slammed to the ground by five Hawk players and pounded on until others came to his rescue. The benches emptied and an out-and-out brawl ensued at the fifty-yard line. Dick hobbled over to stand by Brian. The bigger guys enjoyed slapping helmets with open hands directly over the ear holes, causing a kind of pressure shock to the head. The best place to land punches was in the soft tissue between the groin and the shoulder pads. Buckley and Hudson stood shoulder to shoulder, bashing any Hawk who came near them. They got proficient at popping chinstraps so they could smash bare faces. They seemed to enjoy themselves. A few players used their helmets as clubs by gripping them by the face guard. Getting whacked in the head with a helmet was brain scrambling enough with a helmet on, but those swinging their helmets soon learned that it was much safer to keep their helmets on.

Fans from both sides ran out onto the field to help stop the fighting, but before long, they too were shoving and pushing. The referees tried to bring the game under control, all of them blowing relentlessly on their whistles, but after a while they left the field in disgust. A couple of sheriff deputies attempted to break up the fight but found it hopeless and merely stood along the sidelines and watched. Coach LeClaire did what he could but soon got into a shouting match with the Bozeman coach. After an exchange of profanities, he flipped the coach the finger and walked off the field. He slumped on the bench and pulled a small bottle from his coat pocket. Leaning back, he openly gulped down the remaining contents of the bottle.

Nobody was able to stop the fight. It just seemed to peter out on its own. Some players were hurt and more and more of those fighting stopped to help the injured. Brian protected his bandaged hand as best he could and did manage to get in a few good punches with his right hand. Dick got busted in the head with a freewheeling helmet and crumpled to the ground. He was about to get clobbered with another blow before, out of nowhere, Buckley stepped in and grabbed the helmet-swinging Hawk in a headlock and punched him in the face. When Buckley let the guy go, the fighting seemed to stop. The players and fans began to move off the field.

As the field cleared, Brian looked for Deanie but couldn't see her among the raucous crowd. Dick was bleeding from his mouth and nose, and Brian helped him up and into the school bus parked behind the goal post. It took several minutes to get the equipment loaded and everyone seated for the ride back to the school. When the bus pulled away from the field and lumbered out onto the graveled road, Brian spotted Deanie's white '51 Chevy parked along the hedge grove that encircled the field. A mysterious, brand-new, candy-apple red Pontiac sat idling directly behind it. As the bus passed by, a numbing surge of panic flooded through Brian as he helplessly watched

Deanie squat down next to the driver-side window to talk with the driver. With eyes wide with fear, he pressed his face to the school bus window, craning his neck to look back at her, watching until he could no longer see her.

Chapter Two

"Oh, God!" Deanie gasped, watching the melee breakout on the field. She stood on the sidelines next to Karen, her best friend and one of the other cheerleaders. She could see Brian swinging wildly and her first impulse was to rush out to help him, but seeing the brutality, she merely stood there, clinging helplessly to Karen until the battle ended.

It occurred to her that the whole day had been crazy, starting with the embarrassment she felt over what happened with Brian the night before. Then it was the phone call she received that morning from an old boyfriend, and now, the fight on the field. To make matters worse, a mysterious new Bonneville Pontiac was cruising around on the gravel road alongside the field, the overhead lights shimmering menacingly across its brilliant red finish.

"That's him, isn't it?" Karen asked during halftime.

"Probably," Deanie said, nervously chewing gum. "He likes nice cars."

When she saw the car, her heart began to race. His return to Livingston presented a problem—a problem on top of the problem she already had with Brian. She thought she should be angry with Brian, but she wasn't sure that was the way she really felt. She loved him, but going all the way was not supposed to happen—not then, anyway. He was like her father: handsome, strong, and in charge. Jovial and fun, most of the time, he treated her respectfully. He was protective of her, yet there was a possessiveness about him that frightened her, almost to the point of suffocation. He carried a strange sadness within him, and although he tried his best to conceal it, she felt a need to console him. He needed her and that was what she cherished most. They had gotten together through Karen, who was already going steady with Dick Dana. On a double date, they took an instant liking to one another. By the summer's end, they too were going steady.

Deanie's early-morning phone call was from Bill Slater. He lived in California and visited Livingston each fall to go elk hunting with his uncle.

He was a few years older than Deanie and well out of high school. Hearing his voice again made her feel suddenly excited and afraid at the same time. He was very charming, and Deanie pictured his good looks and neat clothes. She met him two years before, at a Civic Center dance. It was a thrill to have an older guy interested in her. He was charming, polite, and respectful, and she was delighted to see him the next year. Her girlfriends envied her and it flattered her that he picked her and not any of them. But he became angry with her when he left Livingston last year, and Deanie wasn't sure he ever wanted to see her again. Now, when he asked to see her that night, she almost agreed. It was only when she was about to hang up the phone that she came to her senses and managed to blurt out, "No, I can't, Bill. I'm going with someone else now."

When the fighting stopped, everyone began moving away from the field. The night air was cold against their bare legs, and Deanie and Karen hurried off across the field to Deanie's Chevy coupe.

"I hope our guys are okay," Deanie said. She reached for her purse, tucked under the front seat, to retrieve her car keys. "They were all bandaged up even before the fight."

"I just can't believe it," Karen said. "They almost won that game."

The Chevy sputtered a couple of times but started faithfully. The heater was already turned up full blast and Deanie endured the rush of cold air, wishing the warmth would come soon. She looked back across the field at the people still scurrying off to their cars.

"Wonder where the girls are," she said.

"Who knows," Karen said, shivering. "It's Colleen's birthday. I'm sure their minds are on partying."

Deanie had driven all of her girlfriends to the game with the understanding that they were going on to the school dance, before going out to celebrate Colleen's seventeenth birthday. The six of them had been in their group since junior high, when Colleen decided that a girls-only club was a good idea. Deanie was asked in by Karen, who was instrumental in helping Colleen get things organized. Eventually, Linda, Sherry, and Rita joined in. At least once a week, they would hold a get-together at one of their houses to talk about family, school, or boys and who was going with whom. When they reached high school, they would meet before school athletic games at pitch-ins, where their discussions were almost exclusively about guys.

Colleen came up with the name for their club. "Came to me in a dream," she said one day. "Since we're all beautiful, I think we should call ourselves the La Belle Six. It has a sexy French sound, don't you think?"

They all liked the name. From then on, each one of them would be forever enshrined into La Belle Six, a group of attractive, immensely popular girls, each one of them enviously tagged as one of the Belles.

Just before the football team pulled away from the field, the red Pontiac suddenly appeared behind Deanie's Chevy. From her rearview mirror, Deanie saw the confident, smiling face of Bill Slater. He was smoking a cigarette and a river of smoke flowed from his window. He hadn't lost his good looks, although he wore his dark curly hair a bit longer. He wasn't alone in his car.

"Surprise, surprise," Karen said. "There are all the missing Belles, sitting comfortably in a nice, warm car."

Deanie felt her face flush with the first glimpse of Bill Slater. Suddenly, she remembered what she did the previous year, the night before Bill left back to California, when he talked her into showing him what she looked like without any clothes on. They were at Bill's uncle's house, listening to music and necking. Deanie had taken a few drinks of Bill's beer, and after severe pressure from Bill she agreed to bare it all for him, but only if she stood in the doorway of the bathroom, a considerable distance from Bill and where she could quickly slam and lock the door if he dared come near her. Inevitably, Bill did make a grab for her, but she managed to get the door locked before he could reach her. Bill banged on the bathroom door for twenty minutes, pleading for her to let him in. Angry, he finally gave up and Deanie was able to escape from the house. Bill left the next day without saying goodbye. Deanie soon realized it had been a stupid thing to do, and she was ashamed for doing it, yet she still liked Bill. She wrote to him for a few months, but he never answered. When Brian came into her life, she became increasingly preoccupied, and Bill Slater became a thing of the past.

Now Bill was back and apparently as persistent as ever. He honked the horn a few times, but Deanie sat frozen in her Chevy.

"I'll go get them," Karen said, rushing out of the car.

Deanie watched Karen in her rearview mirror. To her bewilderment, Karen had climbed inside with the rest of the Belles. Bill's horn continued to beep, and Deanie finally realized the only way she was going to retrieve her fares was to go and usher them back herself. Cautiously, she approached Bill's Pontiac.

"Hi, beautiful," Bill said, smiling confidently. He draped his arm across the steering wheel, exposing a gold charm bracelet.

"Your car sure is nice, Bill," Deanie said, squatting down, looking inside at Sherry, Linda, and Rita in the back seat, while Karen and Colleen sat up front.

Colleen was busy with the radio dial. Except for Karen's cheerleader outfit, the rest wore colorful sweaters and tight-fitting slacks.

"Don't you think we should get on to the dance?" Deanie asked.

"Dance, are you kidding me?" Bill said mockingly. "Who'd want to go to a boring school dance when we could all ride around in my new car and party all night?

Deanie looked at Karen to make eye contact. Oddly, she did feel tempted to get inside. Karen didn't say anything.

Suddenly, Deanie heard the roar of the school bus as it turned out onto the gravel road.

"It's so warm and nice in here," Sherry said. "Let's go for a ride."

Bill looked out at Deanie. "Wow," he said. "I can't believe it. I've got all the Belles right here. Get in, Deanie."

Deanie felt embarrassed, watching them glare at her. Clearly, they all wanted to go. She considered it for a moment, but even though it might not cause any harm, she still found the courage to shake her head no.

Linda leaned across the back seat to talk out the window. "Come on, Deanie. Brian doesn't even have to know."

Finally, Karen spoke out. "No, Deanie's going steady now. It's not right for her to be riding around with Bill."

Deanie started back toward her car and Karen stepped out of the Pontiac. The others lingered for a time.

Then Colleen blurted out, "Hey, wait a second. Today's my birthday, and we're the Belles. We've got to stick together."

When Colleen stepped out, so did the rest of them.

"What is this?" Bill shouted.

Linda was a little hesitant, but she eventually left, too.

Once the girls were all loaded into Deanie's Chevy, Bill gave a long, irritating blast on his horn.

"Okay, Deanie!" he shouted from his window. "I'll look for you later."

Bill backed his car up and then slammed the shift lever forward, bolting the car out across the gravel road, its back tires spinning and pelting Deanie's car with rocks.

Chapter Three

The smell of the locker room hadn't changed in all the four years Brian had been there. From the very first day, it reeked of musty socks, disinfectant, and rubbing alcohol.

"All your gear must be turned in to the equipment room!" the trainer called out, his voice resounding through the steamy tile-lined shower. "Uniforms and whites go in the laundry room!"

Spirits remained high as the Rangers undressed and showered. The ranting about the Hawks continued as they washed off their cuts, the tile floor running red with blood. There was also the usual ass grabbing and towel snapping, with the upperclassmen doing better than average terrorizing the younger fellows. Hudson held one screaming, naked sophomore in a full nelson while Buckley threatened to grab his testicles.

"With this one iron fist," Buckley said, sneering, "I could pop your nuts like two little grapes."

Brian stood in front of his locker, struggling to re-bandage his finger. He couldn't get his mind off the sight of Deanie talking to the driver of the fancy red Pontiac. His finger ached, but as long as pressure was applied, the bleeding stopped. Dick finally limped over to him to help with the bandage. After getting back into his white t-shirt and Levi's, Brian began cleaning out his locker. A season's accumulation of personal items cluttered the top shelf, including a past-due library book, old exam papers, and several notes from Deanie. Feeling depressed, he unzipped his duffel bag and began filling it. When done, he leaned up against his locker door to wait for Dick to finish dressing. He wished he could be more like Dick. He never seemed to get depressed. Dick pretty much accepted life as it was dealt him. They had been friends since the sixth grade after the Northern Pacific transferred Dick's father in from Minnesota to work the roundhouse. Back then, they were both about the same size, but each year Dick grew taller. Before long, even the uniforms seemed to look better on Dick.

Dick's ankle looked swollen, but he managed to pull on his black loafer. Brian helped him to his feet. He swung his letterman's jacket across his shoulder and swatted Brian on the back. Smiling, he said, "Well, then, ole buddy. What's it going to be, wine, women, or my songs?"

Brian laughed. "Well, at least the first two." He knew how things usually went. They'd start out together for the wine or beer part but ended up going separate ways when the women part started.

"Buckley says he's got a couple of kegs of beer," Dick said, smiling. "Says there's going to be a kegger up on the Point. Want to go?"

"Maybe. I'll see after I talk to Deanie."

With Dick limping, they pushed open the locker room door and headed down the hallway toward the girls' gym, where the school dance was being held, the metal cleats on the heels of their loafers clicking like tap shoes on the polished gray marble floor.

Chapter Four

By the time the Belles got back to the school, the best parking spots near the school were already taken. Deanie had to park two blocks away. They all ran in the chilly air to keep warm. A four-man band was set up under one of the basket hoops, and they were already banging out their renditions of the popular rock and-roll tunes. Mr. Kyle, the music teacher, wasn't as strict as other school chaperons and had allowed the overhead lights to be turned off, leaving only the dim lights along the walls on, giving some atmosphere to the otherwise gloomy facility. Surprisingly, the dance floor was crowded. It wasn't long before the La Belles were asked out on the floor to jitterbug. Linda seemed to be having the most fun, swinging her hips wildly, seemingly delighted in flaunting her curvaceous figure.

Deanie and Karen held back their enthusiasm. When a couple of juniors asked them out on the dance floor, Deanie and Karen twirled in their colorful purple and gold cheerleader outfits but couldn't bring themselves to make the moves Linda made. Deanie still didn't know what she was going to do about Brian. She shuddered again, thinking about what had happened. The football players were slow to trickle into the gym. When they did, it didn't take long for the news about the kegger to leak out.

Shortly after, Brian walked up to her, reaching out for her and pulling her tightly against him. He was careful to hold his bandaged hand to the side. "You've been avoiding me all day," he said, kissing her gently on her neck.

The band played a slower song and Brian walked Deanie out onto the dance floor. Again, he pressed her closely, swaying to the music.

"How's your hand?" Deanie asked. "I worried when I saw you getting bandaged up.

"It hurts a little, but it'll heal."

"That was quite a battle tonight. You guys played your hearts out."

"Yeah," Brian said. "I really wanted to win that game. What's sad about it is the fact that I'll never get other chance."

Deanie turned and kissed him on the mouth.

"You sure smell good," Brian said. "It's kind of like a mixture of lipstick, perfume, and spearmint gum."

Deanie laughed. "That's good to hear," she said. "I worried that I'd smell all sweaty."

"Well, haven't you been avoiding me?"

Deanie pulled back from him. "Oh, Brian, I love you, but it wasn't right what happened last night. We just have to stay away from each other, at least for a while."

"Don't say that, Deanie. I can't stay away from you. I promise it won't happen again."

Deanie shook her head. "You can't promise something like that. And it isn't just you. I can't trust myself."

Brian kissed her on the check. "Come out with me tonight, Deanie."

"I better not, Brian. Besides, it's Colleen's birthday. The Belles promised to all stay together tonight."

They remained quiet until the music stopped and then moved off the dance floor. Deanie sensed his disappointment. Across the gym, Deanie saw Karen and Dick holding on to each other and kissing. They seemed very passionate, and she wondered how Karen managed to hold Dick back.

Brian gave her a long kiss on the mouth. Before he left, he asked about the owner of the red Pontiac.

Deanie felt embarrassed but did her best to make light of the question. "He was just someone I used to know, a long time ago."

"So what did he want?" Brian asked, his breathing becoming quicker.

Deanie shrugged. "He wanted the Belles to go for a ride in his new car. I told him I couldn't go."

"So did he buy that?"

"I think so," Deanie said. "He stormed away mad."

"Can I trust you, Deanie?"

Deanie saw the fear in Brian's eyes. She clasped his hand tightly. "I love you, Brian. Yes, you can."

Deanie smiled at him, and he kissed her one last time before moving off across the gym to find Dick.

Chapter Five

It was ten-thirty when Brian and Dick left the dance. The cold west wind had picked up. The moon was now a soft glow in the western sky. Brian tossed his duffel bag in the back seat of his blue four-door '51 Chevy. He reached across the torn seat cover to unlock the passenger door.

Dick didn't have a car of his own. Brian's Chevy wasn't fancy, but it was the only set of wheels they had. It still sported the large dent on the trunk lid it suffered when Brian's boss, Orlen Picard, helped push Brian out of a snowdrift the previous winter. Orlen's Standard Oil bulk truck managed to get the Chevy out of the drift, but the truck's bumper slipped over the car bumper and the truck slammed into the trunk lid. Orlen said he was sorry, and Brian was quick to make light of the mishap. "One more dent won't make any difference," he said, but felt badly about his car.

Brian turned the key in the ignition. He had to choke it a little, but the Chevy started promptly. He was feeling terrible about Deanie. "I think I need to get drunk," he said.

"What's wrong now?" Dick asked. He was playing with the radio dial. KPRK, the local radio station, had gone off the air and Dick was trying to bring in a Salt Lake station. "You act like you've been gut shot."

"It feels like I have."

An Elvis song came through for a couple seconds but faded out.

"Don't let these women get to you like this, Brian. All they are are prick teasers."

Something was telling him Dick was right, but something else—something stronger—wouldn't or couldn't allow him to accept it. Again, he wished he could be more like Dick.

Brian made a right turn at the corner and drove down Calendar Street. He glanced down at the gas gauge and wondered if the Chevy would make it to

15

the station. The residential streets were dark and deserted, but ahead he saw the neon lights of downtown.

"Something happened last night," Brian said softly, reluctantly. "I shouldn't tell, but I'm about to go crazy."

"Yeah?" Dick said in a surprised voice. "What?"

"I got a little too fresh with Deanie."

Dick's eyes brightened. "You screwed her, didn't you?"

Brian shifted nervously in the car seat. "Well, I guess so. But it was like an accident or something."

Dick let out a war whoop, his face in full grin. "Wow! This is great."

"I thought it was great for a while, just about the most exciting thing that's ever happened. But Deanie started crying right afterward and didn't stop until I took her home. Now she says we shouldn't see each other anymore."

Brian pulled up to the stoplight at the corner of Calendar and Second streets. It always amazed him how different downtown became on the weekend nights. It seemed as though someone forgot to turn off the lights when the customers and shop owners all left. Under the brightly colored neon, Livingston's youths seemed to take over the town, orbiting the two blocks between Main and Second streets in cars and pickups, new and old. Stoplights on each corner slowed traffic, making it easy to leisurely chat with the occupants of the vehicles circling from the other direction. The downtown sounds were a confused muddle of revving engines, shouts, whistles, and the rumble of glass-packed mufflers. Most of the faces were familiar and everyone waved as they passed by. But then, disturbingly, the mysterious shiny red Pontiac passed by, right in front of Brian's Chevy. When the light changed, Brian turned the corner and followed in line behind it.

Brian's pulse quickened. "Well, well," he said, noticing the California plates.

"This must be the big bad wolf, huh?" Dick said, chuckling.

"Yes, it is," Brian said, slowly nodding his head.

Just then, a soft girl's voice spoke from a crowded blue '54 Ford, barely moving next to them. Her name was Julie Stephens. "Hi, Brian and Dick," she said. "Great fight tonight."

"Hi, Julie. Yeah, we got a few licks in."

"Going to the kegger?" she asked.

"Yeah, probably. Say, do you know the dude in the red Pontiac?"

Julie's car started forward and Brian could hear giggles from the back seat. "No," Julie said, grinning. "But we would like to."

Dick poked Brian in the ribs. "You're good at this sort of things now," he said in a whisper. "Ask her if she wants to fuck."

Brian turned and gave Dick a quick swat across his chest.

The red Pontiac continued to cruise around the block, and Brian stayed close to his bumper.

"I should wave this guy down and have a little talk with him," Brian said, glancing again at the gas gauge. "But we're about to run out of gas." Brian broke ranks and headed east on Park Street. "I'll have to catch up to him later," he said. "Hope we make it to the station."

Park Street was also Highway 89, which ran parallel to the railroad tracks. The station sat on the corner of Park and I streets. It was a square flat-roofed building with three pumps out front, two regular and one premium. Its blue and-white stucco siding matched the colors of the high Standard Oil sign that towered above it next to the highway. The station had a total of five rooms: the office, the service bay room with its one hydraulic hoist, a small adjoining tire and tube room, the ladies' restroom, and the men's room just off the office. Orlen Picard owned the station along with the Standard Oil bulk plant at the end of the street. Brian had worked there off and on over the past two years, working summers, weekends, after school, and after football practices.

Brian's Chevy ran out of gas one block too soon, but the wind was blowing at its normal blustery pace, allowing Brian to merely throw the car into neutral, letting the wind propel them the rest of the way in. The Chevy glided easily up next to the pumps. Once stopped, Brian noticed a new metallic-gold Chrysler parked alongside the station.

"Man, who belongs to that?" Dick asked.

"Don't know," Brian said. "I'll get the pumps switched on. Go ahead and fill her up."

Brian unlocked the front door and stepped inside. The air felt even cooler than outside. He switched on the overhead light and read a note taped to the cash register. He clicked on the pump switch and watched Dick begin filling the gas tank. The note was from Orlen, telling Brian what needed to be done over the weekend. With the Chevy filled up, Brian wrote up a ticket for the gas and switched everything off.

"Found out whose car that is," Brian said, scooting in under the steering wheel.

"Yeah?" Dick said. "Probably belongs to one rich son-of-a-bitch, right?"

Brian laughed. "You could say that. It belongs to Charlotte Burk."

"Okay, who's Charlotte Burk?"

"She's the madam out at the cathouse," Brian said, grinning.

"You're kidding, right?"

"Nope, and get this. I have to deliver it out there after I finish servicing it."

Dick let out one of his war whoops.

Chapter Six

Harvat's Flat is a windswept plain, rising sharply from the valley floor of the Yellowstone River and gently sloping upward toward the timbered hills and rocky peaks of the Absaroka Mountains. The flat is covered in native grasses that sway harmoniously in voracious winds that roar in from both the south and the west, colliding with the force of two freight trains. To get up there from town, one must take the highway east across the river for a couple of miles and then a graveled back road that eventually jackknifes upward and out onto the flat. On top, a road leads to a place that became known as the Point, a narrow rocky strip of unwanted land, hanging between sheer cliffs on its north and riverside and a deep ravine at its south. In daylight, the Point is a great place to watch for free the annual Livingston rodeo and other functions held at the fairgrounds. Across the river and out of the city limits, it's a place to shoot off fireworks, a place to just sit in a car to talk, dream, or listen to the radio. It is a great place to drink beer and to neck. Usually, most things done there are best done at night, under the cover of darkness.

From this windy knoll, one can glimpse the entire town of Livingston, sprawling north to south along the Yellowstone River, and nestled between the rolling bald bluffs to the north and the tree-covered mountains to the south. The Northern Pacific mainline leaves the bridge crossing, skirts the bluffs, and eventually disappears into the mountains to the west. A branch line follows the river southward through the mountains on its way to Yellowstone National Park. Livingston's most distinguishing features include a brick smokestack near the center of town, towering above the railroad shops. On the face of the north-side hill are two gigantic whitewashed stone designs—one, the likeness of a rainbow trout, frozen in time as if leaping from the water; the other, the letter P representing Park County High School.

Brian was amazed to see so many people dashing about a blazing bonfire near the cliff edge, its flames shooting high into the dark sky and seemingly fluttering away in the wind. He found a place to park along the road. Ahead, he could see Dan Buckley's red '49 Ford pickup positioned near the fire with two sixteen-gallon beer kegs resting on the ground behind the truck. Ray Hudson sat on the tailgate with his leg plopped over one of the kegs, while a half circle of eager bodies, paper cups in hand, waited like tramps in a food line for a turn at the spigot.

"Man, you should have driven up here in Buckley's truck," said one of the already inebriated lettermen in line. "The bastard scared the crap out of us. He guns it at the turn of the switchback and bounces Timmy McCoy out the back of the pickup. Doesn't even stop to pick him up. Timmy had to limp in the rest of the way. Then Buckley streaks off, straight for the cliff edge, screaming, 'No brakes!' The crazy loon slams on his brakes at the very last second."

"Sounds like a typical Buckley party to me," Dick said, smiling.

"It's about time you two showed up," Ray Hudson scolded when they reached the head of the line.

"How much is the beer, Ray?" Brian asked.

Hudson hadn't bothered using a cashbox but merely stuffed the money he collected in his letterman's jacket. "Beer's free. Cups are a buck apiece."

With their cups filled, Brian and Dick found a place at the fire. They sat on the rocky ground, where they could look out over the lights of town. A discussion was already in progress about an incident that happened on the Point a few years before. The whole town was stunned to learn that the car two young lovers were in toppled over the cliff's edge, killing them both.

"Suicide, my ass," Buckley blurted out, tossing another broken branch on the fire. "I'll bet the guy was trying to bang her and accidentally kicked the car out of gear with his foot. Hell, he probably had it in her when the car went over the ledge."

Brian looked back toward the road and shuddered. The land looked flat but did gradually slope toward the cliff's edge. In the dark, without trees or even large rocks, it would be easy to not sense a slight rolling motion, especially if your mind was on other things.

Dick finished his beer and started back to the pickup for another. "Can you see the cathouse from up here?"

Brian stood up, looking off to the north. "Yeah," he said, pointing. "See the pink porch light?"

"You ever see this Charlotte?" Dick asked.

Brian shook his head. "She's a new customer."

"When you deliver her car tomorrow, ask her if she'll let us in sometime."

Brian laughed. "I doubt she will. I think they require you to be twenty-one."

"There's something all wrong with the system we have," Dick growled. "Guys our age would keep those places rolling in dough."

Guys and girls continued to arrive and to crowd around the fire. Brian kept hoping the Belles would decide to come. Julie Stephens and her friends came up. They seemed to enjoy bending over in their tight slacks to warm their backsides.

The underclassmen had been given the job of starting and keeping the fire going. They made several trips down the ravine to gather tree limbs. Later, a couple of seniors became disgusted with their puny fire and hauled up a twenty-foot windfall. They doused it with gas from one of the gas cans Buckley carried in his truck bed and abruptly tossed it across the flames.

Buckley was busy necking with one of the sophomore girls, and when the flames shot up, he leaped up, shouting, "Holy shit! You'll have the sheriff up here for sure."

The guys' pissing spot was on the other side of the Point, where they could pee over the ledge. A couple of underclassmen were leaning against one of the parked cars when Brian came near.

"Hey, West," one of them said. "Did you notice all the headlights flashing around over on the north-side hill?"

Brian stepped up to relieve himself and looked to the northwest. He felt a little wobbly from the beer. "You mean by the P?"

"Yeah. Must be five or six different rigs up there. Jack Wheeler and some guys just took off to check it out. Do you suppose someone is messing around with the P?"

Brian finished buttoning his Levi's. He remembered his boss, Orlen, telling him how in the old days, Bozeman kids would sneak over every now and then and rearrange the whitewashed stones into the letter B.

Back at the fire, the heat had caused everyone to move away some. Most were getting drunk and the laughter had increased. Buckley was huddled under a blanket with his sophomore girlfriend. Dick had limped off to the other side of the fire to chat with Julie Stephens, and Brian suddenly felt depressed. He thought about Deanie, closing his eyes, trying to visualize the night before. Sadly, he had no mental picture of what had happened, but he remembered the touch and smell of her. He loved her and he was glad it happened. He wondered about the future. He'd be out of school in the spring. What he would do after that, he had no idea. He rested back on his elbows and looked west. The lights didn't taper gradually away but seemed to end abruptly at the edge of town. Beyond, there was nothing but a vast, cold darkness.

Chapter Seven

When Deanie left the dance, all she really wanted to do was to go home—and she would have if Karen hadn't insisted she go with the Belles to celebrate Colleen's birthday. Since Colleen's '56 Ford was much roomier, Deanie left her car at the school. Sherry and Linda sat up front with Colleen, while Karen, Rita, and Deanie sat in the backseat. Usually, it was fun circling the drag, enjoying the attention they got—especially from the guys, who shouted and waved at them. But now, Deanie slouched low in the seat, fearful of meeting up with either Brian or Bill.

"I love it when we can all be together," Colleen said, smiling and glancing in her rearview mirror at her friends. "All we have to do is get Deanie cheered up."

"Yeah," Linda blurted out, laughing. "Let's hold her down and get her drunk."

"I say we get updated on the contest," Rita said boldly.

Sherry turned around to look back at Rita. "Uh-oh," she uttered merrily." Sounds like someone has something to tell us."

The contest was something Linda came up with their junior year to decide which one of them was the best lover. The Belle who had felt the most penises by graduation would be the winner. Sherry came up with the motto: "Squeeze 'em and please 'em." It was established early that the penises had to be touched bare and not through clothing. They all laughed at Karen when she asked one day if the penises had to be stiff.

"If they aren't stiff by the time you feel them," Colleen offered, grinning, "they shouldn't be counted anyway."

Only Linda confessed that she wasn't a virgin any longer. She enjoyed talking about the fling she had that past summer with a soldier passing through Livingston on his way to Fort Lewis. She left a Civic Center dance with him one Saturday night, rode around town for a while, and then ended up in his room at the Murray Hotel.

"At least I didn't do it in the back seat of a car," she boasted.

Deanie couldn't talk about what had happened with Brian. She could tell Karen, but she wasn't ready to divulge it to everyone—not yet, anyway. "It was kind of sneaky how it all happened," she told Karen. "We were lying down, making out. I had my panties on, but Brian managed to slide up under the leg band. He caught me completely off guard."

All it took to get the booze was for Linda to make a phone call to her brother, Greg, who worked as a janitor at the Mint Bar. They would park in the alley behind the bar and wait. But waiting for Greg was somewhat nerve wracking. Should a police car come along, there wasn't any good reason for them to be sitting in a dark alley with the lights off and the car running.

After what seemed like an eternity, Greg finally opened the back door of the bar, throwing a bright light across a narrow unpaved parking lot and causing each girl to slide down in the car seats. Greg was tall and thin and wore a brown apron over a white shirt and jeans. He closed the door and carried a large garbage can over next to a row of barrels. Before emptying the can, he made a quick look around and removed a brown sack from the inside the garbage can. He held the package close to his side and casually strolled over to Colleen's car. He reached his head inside next to Colleen and handed the package off to Linda. Smiling, he said, "Hope you all like lime-flavored vodka."

While it was illegal to drink anywhere under the age of twenty-one, it was a lot safer to drink on the outskirts of town. With only a few patrol cars, the sheriff's office had a much wider area to patrol than the city police. One of the Belles' favorite places was the seldom used Willow Creek Road, just east of town. The local whorehouse was along the way, and it was usually Linda who insisted they pull into the parking lot for a few minutes just to see who might be visiting. She had an obsession with the white stucco house with its tightly drawn red curtains and its brightly glowing pink porch light. Once, they had parked in the back of the unlit lot and spotted Mr. Kyle's gray Plymouth parked up close to the house. They left before he came out, but Deanie remembered feeling embarrassed seeing Mr. Kyle in the school halls the following Monday.

Linda had the cap off the vodka bottle even before they passed the city limits sign. Each of girls had gulped down two mouthfuls by the time they reached the whorehouse road. Colleen pulled into the parking lot before Linda had a chance to make her plea.

The cars weren't recognizable, mostly licensed in Bozeman and Billings.

Linda giggled. "Just imagine what's happening in there."

"I don't get girls who work in places like that," Rita said. "They must have to do it with any dirty old guy."

Linda had just finished taking another drink from the bottle. "I think it's kind of exciting," she said, grinning and wiping some dribble from her chin.

"My dad thinks whorehouses are good," Sherry spoke up. "He says they keep the perverts satisfied and the streets safer."

Deanie sat quietly in the back seat. She had taken three swigs from the bottle already and hadn't felt much change in her mood.

"Did you know," Linda began confidently, "some of the whores are married?"

"Now how would you know about that?" Colleen was quick to challenge.

"They even keep photos of their husbands right on the nightstands next to them where they do it."

"All right, Linda," Karen interrupted rudely. "How do you know all this stuff? Have you been in there?"

Linda's eyes brightened. "No, but my brother, Greg, has. He told me all about it."

By the time they had reached Willow Creek Road, all of them were feeling the vodka. Even Deanie was now feeling a gentle numbness in her arms and legs.

"So tell us what else your brother told you," Colleen said, her face now locked in a perpetual grin.

"Well," Linda gladly went on, "some of it is kind of nasty."

"Yes," Colleen quizzed. "Go on." She had driven past the Willow Creek Bridge and turned down a narrow-rutted road that led to a grove of aspen trees. With her car completely concealed among the aspens, she stopped and switched off the lights.

"Every room is dimly lit in soft pink light," Linda continued. "And the air is very heavy with sweet-smelling perfume."

"How many times has he been there?" Sherry asked.

"He and his friends go there a lot. He said the girls are kind of young but not very pretty."

"That's probably why they whore themselves," Karen said. "They can't get guys any other way."

"Maybe so, but my brother said they sure can give the guys a swell time."

Each girl was quiet for a time, drinking and passing along the bottle. They took turns going out to the back of the car to pee. Deanie felt lightheaded and rested back against the seat. She looked off down Willow Creek, thinking she saw a flash of light, but after looking alertly for another minute, she never saw the light again. Listening to Linda prattle on about the whores, she thought about what she had done with Brian. All her life, her mother harped about having sex before marriage. Yet the whores and even Linda seemed so carefree about the subject. To them, staying virgin wasn't any big thing.

No one saw or heard the car pull up behind them. It had its lights off. The only reason they sensed it was even there was when the bumpers met and jarred Colleen's car. Colleen had the bottle in her hand at the time. The bump was enough to splatter a little of the vodka against the dashboard. Suddenly, a whirling red light lit up the darkness.

"Damn, it's the cops!" Colleen shouted, frantically searching the front seat for the bottle cap.

"Hide the booze!" Karen yelled.

Colleen couldn't find the cap and merely placed the bottle behind her back and pressed against it. "Everyone, be quiet," she said. "And act sober."

All of them kept their eyes fixed straight ahead, afraid to even turn around to look, waiting for a uniform to appear at the door.

After a time, Colleen dared to glance in the rearview mirror. "No one is getting out of the car," she whispered.

The spinning red light illuminated the inside of the car, and Deanie saw the frightened faces of her friends, each nervously chewing their gum. She envisioned all of them being handcuffed and carted off to jail. There wasn't anything they could do, except try and make a break for it.

Finally, after what seemed like several minutes, Deanie forced herself to turn around and look out the rear window. "Something's kind of strange about this," she said. "The red light is flashing from inside the car, not on top."

Everyone turned to look and saw that the light appeared to be coming from a mount on the dashboard.

"I think we've been had," Rita was quick to say. "It's not the cops."

Colleen shouted, "Lock the doors! We're getting out of here!"

Ahead, the road meandered through the trees for several yards before bending back toward the main road. Colleen pressed down on the accelerator and never looked back. She made the bend and was headed back before anyone realized the strange car hadn't given chase. It merely sat unmoving in the middle of the road, its phony red light still whirling from its dashboard. Colleen had to slam on her brakes to avoid ramming into its front bumper.

"Oh, my God!" Sherry screamed. "It's Bill Slater!"

With the headlights glaring in his eyes, Bill Slater got out of his Pontiac, laughing. He leaned against his front fender and took a drink from his beer can.

"You bastard!" Colleen called out.

Karen was the first to leap out of Colleen's Ford, running up to Bill and shoving him. "What the hell are you doing, scaring us like that?"

Bill continued to laugh, holding his arms out to protect himself. He reached inside the Pontiac and switched off the spinning red light. "We play that trick a lot in California."

All of the Belles scampered from Colleen's car. None of them could see the humor in the trick.

"Move your damn car so we can get out of here," Colleen demanded.

Bill gulped down the last of his beer and tossed the can off into the darkness. He stood, smiling at them. "I want to talk to Deanie," he said.

"Well, she doesn't want to talk to you," Karen said sharply.

Deanie was shivering. She wasn't sure it was from the cold or from fear. She wished she had changed out of her cheerleader's skirt. Frustrated, she called out to Bill, "I can't be with you now, Bill. I told you I was going with someone else."

All the Belles began to move in close to Deanie, surrounding her in a kind of protective huddle.

"Come sit in my car for a minute, Deanie. I just want to talk with you."

Deanie made a slight move toward Bill's car, but Karen grabbed her arm.

"Don't do it, Deanie."

"If I talk to him a minute, maybe he'll go away and leave me alone. You guys are right here."

"Are you sure, Deanie?" Colleen asked, sounding concerned.

"It'll be okay," Deanie said. Again, she moved toward Bill's car, with her friends all reluctant to let her go.

Deanie quickly stepped around Bill and opened the driver's door to the Pontiac. The interior light cast a soft glow as Deanie scooted across the black leather seats. The warm air had a smell of newness. The radio was coming in clearly. Roy Orbison was singing *"Only the Lonely."* She wondered if the new cars had better radios. Outside, she watched her friend's pace nervously in front of the Pontiac.

The first thing Bill Slater did when he got inside the car was to reach around and lock all the doors. "Man," he said. "You have some kind of gang here."

The very next thing Bill did was to jam the shift lever into reverse and stomp down on the gas pedal. The Pontiac bolted backward, spewing up dirt and small rocks. Bill didn't switch on the headlights until he made it to the main road.

Deanie screamed, "Stop! What are you doing?"

Bill spun the Pontiac around and headed back down Willow Creek Road. Deanie heard rocks banging beneath them as they picked up speed. Behind them, Colleen's Ford had made it to the main road, but it was obvious they weren't going to catch up.

Chapter Eight

Jack Wheeler's '52 Mercury almost slammed into Buckley's pickup when it arrived back from investigating the strange lights flashing over the north-side hill. Jack was shouting even before he got the car stopped. "The 'P' is all fucked up!"

Buckley was sitting quietly on the ground, cuddled up with his girlfriend when he heard Wheeler roar in. "It's the Hawks," Buckley bellowed, his gold teeth glistening in the firelight. He looked more thrilled than angry. He leaped up into the bed of his pickup. "Those bastards have come over here and messed up our 'P'!" he shouted, while the partygoers circled his pickup.

"Looks like you've been replaced at quarterback," Dick chuckled to Brian.

Buckley continued to rant. "Are we going to let them get away with this?"

A chorus of "no" answered him and Buckley gave a one-fisted charge signal.

"Let's go 'P' their football field!" he shouted.

Suddenly, there was a scramble to get to the vehicles. Ray Hudson pushed the kegs and box of paper cups to the back of the pickup bed and slammed the tailgate. The pickup was promptly loaded with drunken teenagers and led the charge down Harvat's Flat Road.

The air turned thick with dust, and Brian could barely make out the vehicle in front of him. He felt like he was in a stock car race. "I guess the kegger is over," he said to Dick. He listened to the rattle coming from his right-front fender, wondering if it was going to fall off.

"Did you see the fire in Buckley's eyes?" Dick asked. "Is he excited or what?"

Brian kept on the lookout for patrol cars as he sped out onto the highway. At the city limit sign, he slowed. Several cars began to pass them on Park Street.

"I'm not going over to Bozeman," he said with finality.

Dick looked over at him in disbelief. "What, are you kidding me? We have to go."

"This thing with Deanie is getting to me, Dick. I have this awful feeling in my gut. I'm not sure about this California dude."

Dick got quiet. Soon, Julie Stephen's Ford swung around them to pass.

"Get that piece of junk moving!" one of the girls in back shouted out. "We're on our way to kick some ass!"

"Listen," Dick said, "I'd like to know where Karen is, too, but let's do this thing first. Besides, a little action will get your mind off her for a while."

When they passed by the station, Dick craned his neck to gawk once more at the gold Chrysler parked next to the building.

"Tell me, buddy," Dick grinned. "Do you have to clean the pecker tracks off the seat covers when you service her car?"

Brian laughed.

"So, are we going to Bozeman or not?"

Brian hesitated but then finally shrugged. "Yeah, what the hell. Let's go," he said, stomping down on the gas pedal.

Excitedly, Dick began rummaging through the jockey box. "Got any smokes in here? I never agreed much with Buckley on anything," he continued. "But as far as I'm concerned, this is the fifth quarter of the game. They hit us, we hit back."

He found one slightly bent Pall Mall under some papers and lit it with the dashboard lighter. He started coughing almost immediately and handed the glowing cigarette off to Brian. He then took on the task of dialing in a radio station. He had a Salt Lake station for a moment, but it quickly became static.

"We've got to get out of this country," Dick growled, switching the radio off in disgust. "We're so far from civilization, we can't even get radio."

Brian took a drag on the cigarette. "I know," he said, coughing. "You ever wonder what the hell we're going to do after we graduate?"

"Yeah, makes me nervous to think about it. Nothing to do here, really. Maybe the railroad. If I stay in Livingston, I'll probably end up a drunk like my old man."

"Unless I join the Service, I'll probably be pumping gas 'til I'm sixty-five," Brian said.

At the crest of the Bozeman hill, Dick reached over and retrieved the cigarette from Brian. It was about gone, but he managed to get one last long drag from it. "Man," he said. "I can't believe you screwed Deanie."

Brian didn't answer him right away, and Dick quickly added, "Karen won't let me do anything much with her. All she'll do is play with my pecker once in a while. I tell you, buddy, sometimes it gets so hard, I couldn't cut it with a hacksaw."

"I probably shouldn't have told you about it," Brian said.

"What? We're buddies, aren't we? Who the hell else you going to tell, your mother?"

"I wonder why she didn't want to go out with me tonight. You'd think we'd be closer now."

"She's probably a little scared. It only takes one time to get a girl knocked up."

Brian thought for a moment. "I guess I wasn't focused on that at the time."

"I think you've been hit too many times in the head," Dick said, laughing.

The more Dick went on, the more nervous Brian got.

Chapter Nine

Deanie remained pressed against the passenger door of Bill Slater's Pontiac as it sped down Willow Creek Road. She felt better when Bill turned onto the highway and headed toward town. But when he didn't stop in town and kept on driving south along the river, she became frightened once again. She pleaded for Bill to let her out, but he merely ignored her. A radio station was breaking through and she heard the Platters sing "*Smoke Gets in Your Eyes.*" Overhead, the stars were ablaze across a blackened sky.

Bill remained strangely quiet, chain smoking. The tires squealed when they crossed Carter's Bridge, weaving through the long, sweeping curves. At Pine Creek, Bill turned down a dirt road, leading to the river. The road narrowed and rambled among the cottonwoods along the riverbank. Once concealed from the main road, Bill stopped the Pontiac. He switched off the headlights but kept the motor running. A strong wind whipped in among the trees, jarring loose the leaves that rained gently down around the car.

Deanie's heart pounded. She felt hopelessly trapped and braced herself for the struggle to come. She thought about how unfair being a girl was. Being with guys meant holding and kissing them, wanting what they wanted, but always having to fight them off.

Bill sat quietly for a time, listening to the radio and gazing out at the stars. After crushing his cigarette in the dashboard tray, he finally spoke. "What are you going to do after high school, Deanie?" His voice was calm and unthreatening.

Deanie answered cautiously. "I don't really know. Probably find a job in Livingston or Bozeman."

"That sounds so depressing," Bill said, shaking his head.

"There's not much else to do," Deanie said. "I'd like to go to college, but there isn't money for that."

"I want to tell you about this new job I have in LA, Deanie. I started it two years ago. It's a great job and they pay me very well."

"I'm glad for you, Bill."

"There's a place there for you, too, Deanie. Hell, all the Belles would fit in great."

"Sounds wonderful. What kind of job?"

"It's like a modeling agency," Bill said. "They only hire beautiful girls."

Deanie felt flattered, but she sensed she shouldn't trust him.

"Remember that time at my uncle's place, Deanie? I can't get the vision of you naked out of my head."

Deanie shuddered. "It was a stupid thing to do, Bill. I regret it."

"I certainly don't," Bill said. He slid across the seat and put his arm around Deanie's shoulder. "You turn me on, Deanie," he said, leaning to kiss her.

Deanie brought her hands up to meet him.

Bill pressed against her, his breath heavy on her neck. "Come on, kiss me."

"No," Deanie said firmly.

"Just one kiss," Bill pleaded. "Give me something to remember you by."

Deanie realized she was in an awful situation. She sat still. If he was going to kiss her, she wasn't going to help him. Soon, Bill forced his lips hard against her mouth and then buried his head between her neck and shoulder, running his hand across her bare leg an up under her skirt.

"Damn you, Bill!" Deanie shouted, slapping at him. "I can't do this."

"Yes, you can," Bill said, pinning her against the door and holding his forearm to her throat. Only when she began struggling for air did he back off the pressure. "Okay," he said finally. "Just tell me one thing."

Deanie gasped. "What?"

"How far have you and your new boyfriend gone?"

Deanie didn't answer. She felt herself trembling.

Bill grabbed her shoulders and shook her. "Have you gone all the way?" he demanded.

Deanie began to cry. "I love him, Bill."

"So that's it," he bellowed, becoming more and more agitated. "Well, if you did it with him, you're going to do it with me."

Bill forced her down in the seat, working his fingers inside her panties. His weight was crushing. She soon accepted the inevitable and stopped fighting. Most of her clothing came off quickly and she lay helpless in the seat. When she felt his bare skin, she closed her eyes and thought of Brian. The radio was coming in perfectly, but Bill's heavy breathing made it impossible to hear it. He was hurting her, but after a time, it didn't matter anymore. She just wanted it to be over.

Chapter Ten

It was almost one in the morning when the assault team rumbled into Bozeman. Once on Main Street, the gap between vehicles shortened. Traffic was slow and Buckley led the invaders to the school grounds. A high chain-link fence surrounded the dark field, and Buckley positioned his pickup solidly against the gate to test the strength of the lock. His balding tires smoked and spun in the gravel, but the gate held firm. He then backed up twenty yards and revved his motor. When he dropped the clutch, the front wheels came off the ground and the pickup leaped forward, crashing into the gate. Surprisingly, the lock held. What gave way was the fence itself, as several steel posts popped out of the ground and ten feet of fence fell out ahead of Buckley's pickup.

"Wow!" Brian said, following in line with the cars swarming out onto the Hawks' football field. "This is looking kind of serious."

About fifteen vehicles scattered across the field, zigzagging in the drying grass, tearing up large chunks of sod. Buckley stopped his pickup on the fifty-yard line, and like the formation of a huddle, the vehicles all circled around it, their headlights shining like stage lights. Buckley again positioned himself in the truck bed.

Brian looked back at the gate opening, expecting to see police cars. "So, what's he going to have us do now, drop our pants and piss all over the field?"

Dick was totally taken up in the excitement. He hurried out of the car and limped over next to Buckley.

"Okay, here's the plan," Buckley said. "We're going to burn a 'P' in their field. I need two volunteers."

Dick and Jack Wheeler were the first to raise their hands, and Buckley picked them.

"All right, Dana and Wheeler, grab a gas can out of my pickup," Buckley commanded. "All these cars get off the field."

Brian called out to Dick, "You really want me to leave you out here? The cops will be here any minute."

Dick waved. "I'll be fine," he said, grinning. "They can't arrest us all."

"They won't arrest anyone. They'll just start shooting."

Brian drove his Chevy back into the parking lot, parking like everyone else so that his headlights would shine out on the field. He nervously revved his motor, watching the action and listening to Buckley bark out orders.

"Wheeler, you start pouring gas in a straight line from the twenty-yard line until you get to midfield. Dana, as soon as Wheeler finishes, you start drawing out the top of the 'P.' I want the arc to extend from the fifty- to the thirty-yard line."

Brian watched Dick hobble across the field, almost dragging his gas can. He looked the epitome of someone playing hurt. *"Why couldn't Buckley pick someone with two good legs?"*

Wheeler used up his whole can of gas by the time he got to midfield. Dick had plenty to complete the letter "P." When Dick was ready, Buckley shouted for Wheeler to light his match. When he did, a river of flame blazed through the grass, sending thick puffs of smoke into the night air. In a matter of seconds, the visibility on the field became nil.

Brian heard Buckley call out, "Stay where you are, Dana! I'll pick you up after I get Wheeler."

From the surrounding neighborhood, Brian saw a few porch lights flick on. Through the smoke, he saw blurred streaks of Buckley's red pickup dashing about, but he couldn't see Dick anymore.

Soon, the Livingston vehicles began zooming away from the school grounds. Off in the distance, Brian heard the chilling sounds of sirens. For a time, he couldn't see anything out on the field, but then, out of the smoke, Buckley's pickup cannon-balled through the fence opening, snagging the edge of the broken chain-link and causing the pickup to vault upward. When it came down, one of the beer kegs flipped out over the tailgate, landing back on the field. Jack Wheeler was in the pickup bed, along with Ray Hudson and several others, desperately clinging to the side panels, with the other beer keg, boxes of paper cups, and gas cans flying all about them.

Sirens were getting closer, and Dick was nowhere in sight. Brian anxiously flashed his headlights. Then, through a clearing in the smoke, Brian glimpsed Dick at midfield, struggling to run on his bad leg. Without hesitation, Brian hit the gas pedal, catapulting out into the smoke. He saw one city police car in pursuit of Buckley, another was after him. The smoke was so thick, Brian wondered if they actually succeeded in burning a "P" in the grass or simply burned up the entire field. Out on the field, Brian couldn't see anything except the flashing light behind him. At the fifty-yard line, he slowed, hoping Dick would find him. Amazingly he did, jerking open the door and leaping inside.

"That damn Buckley," Dick said, groaning and holding on to his bad leg. "He smacked into me and drove off before I could get in."

"We're in deep shit, buddy," Brian said, jamming the gears. "Hold on!"

The police car was now almost up to them. Brian spun the Chevy around and floor boarded it. Ahead, he saw the opening in the fence, but just before reaching it, his front bumper smacked into something hard. They watched in amazement as one of Buckley's kegs sailed out in front of them, crash landing in the parking lot and spewing beer like a geyser.

Brian made a dash for Main Street. The police car behind him had slowed, and by the time Brian left the school grounds, it was no longer in pursuit. But at Main Street, they saw a few police cars blocking the street ahead.

"We can't get home this way," Brian said. At the corner he made a quick left turn.

"Head north to Bridger Creek!" Dick shouted. "We'll take the back way home."

Bridger Creek Road was mostly unpaved and meandered through the valleys in the Bridger Mountains. When they got to the road, Brian was relieved not to see roadblocks. It would be a longer way home, but safer. There weren't many cars on the road, and they remained vigilant, pulling off the road and hiding among the pine trees whenever headlights appeared. Bridger Creek Road eventually met up with Bracket Creek Road, which took them into Clyde Park and out on Highway 89. From there, they would turn off onto Willow Creek Road and enter Livingston from the north.

"Do you think Buckley got away?" Brian asked. He felt extremely tired. His head throbbed and his mouth was as dry as sagebrush. The rank odor of burned grass lingered, even with the windows open.

"I hope so," Dick said, slumped in the front seat. "He had beer in his pickup. We know he lost one of the kegs. With any luck, he might have lost the other one, too. If anyone can evade the cops, it'd be Buckley." Dick snuggled back against the door, pulling his letterman's jacket up around his ears.

When they drove into Livingston, the sky was changing from black to dark gray. The station had to be opened by six, and Brian wondered if it would even be worth going to bed. Dick lived on the east end, as he did, just two blocks south of the tracks. When Brian finally pulled up in front of Dick's house, Brian had to shake him awake. He got out quickly and was ready to slam the door shut, when he stuck his head back inside.

"Brian," he started to say, pausing. "Thanks for saving my ass, buddy."

When Brian got home, he entered his house through the back door as he always did when he came home late. He never understood why his mother thought it necessary to lock the front door at night and not the back door. If a burglar happened along, he'd probably try the back door first. He didn't bother undressing, merely lying on his bed and using his jacket as a cover. From his window, he looked up at the paling night sky. The wind was strong, and it whistled in through a small crack in the corner of the windowpane. He thought about all that had happened. He wondered what the Hawks' field would look like in the daylight. His finger hurt. Soon he relaxed and his mind drifted to Deanie.

Chapter Eleven

When Bill finished with her, he reached over to the jockey-box. A small light flashed on inside and while Bill searched for a package of tissue, Deanie glimpsed the pearl butt-end of a handgun, holstered in brown leather, lying at the back of the box. The sight of it frightened her even more. It wasn't a western-style gun like the kind her father owned. This one looked more like the kind a gangster would use. She was glad when he finally got off of her. The interior light flashed across him as he stepped outside to dress. Shocked at seeing him naked, Deanie quickly hurried into her own clothes, strewed across the floorboards. Once dressed, she curled up into a ball against the passenger door and cried. She was glad when the interior light went out. The darkness made everything seem less real.

"Now that wasn't so bad, was it?" Bill said.

"Just take me to my car," Deanie snapped at him, wiping her face with the sleeve of her sweater.

Bill lit up another cigarette and shifted the car into reverse. "You're making too much of this, Deanie," he said, backing the Pontiac down the narrow lane. "Accept it for what it was: something wonderful."

She had lost track of the time, but it was early morning when Bill brought her to her car. She could hardly wait to get away from him. Even before the Pontiac had come to a stop, she had the door unlatched, prepared to leap out. Bill said something about calling her, but she didn't answer. She ran to her car. Only with the doors locked did she feel safe. She watched the Pontiac spin off up the darkened street. At the corner, the brilliant red finish reflected the streetlamp and the light flowing over it seemed to shimmer in distorted, menacing waves.

Deanie didn't know what to do. She yearned for the seclusion and safety of her bedroom. Concerned that her friends might still be looking for her, she drove by Colleen's house and saw her Ford parked in the driveway. She wanted to talk with Karen, but all the lights were off in her house. She didn't have the courage to drive by Brian's house. Frightened and confused, she drove home. Home was on the east side, near the river. Her father's pickup wasn't there, as it seldom was. He worked as a brakeman for the Northern Pacific, working westbound freight trains in and out of Livingston. It troubled her how little she got to see him, especially in her high school years. He would be disappointed if he knew what had been happening to her.

A bright yard light lit up the weathered two-story house. A small light shone through the kitchen window. She parked the Chevy in the driveway and ran into the house. She fought back the urge to rush into her mother's bedroom and throw herself into her arms. Instead, she went up to her bedroom. She undressed quickly, tossing her cheerleader's clothes in a pile next to her dresser. Donning a long cotton nightgown, she slid into bed, pulling the covers over her head. She felt a dreadful ache in her side. She cried softly and prayed. Eventually, she persuaded herself not to think about what happened. When sleep finally came, it brought little relief. A dream caused the ache in her side to persist.

In her dream, *she was in a strange new school, a large stone building with many floors and long hallways. It was the beginning of a new school year and there was much excitement as each student, with class schedules and books in hand, rushed through halls to their respective classrooms. Deanie had her schedule clearly written on notebook paper, but as time went by, the schedule became lost and the location of one particular class was forgotten. It was somewhere on an upper floor and Deanie raced frantically between her other classes, searching for it. As each day passed, she became increasingly frustrated. The longer she went without going to class, the more certain she was going to fail. Brian and the Belles were there, genuinely caring and willing to help, but they had their own classes to attend and they had to leave her wandering alone among hundreds of other students dashing about the school. There was a terrible sense of urgency. Time was running out.*

Chapter Twelve

Brian arrived at the station a few minutes before six. If he had gotten any sleep, it certainly didn't feel like it. His mother had awakened him at a quarter to six and he hurried out the door without eating. The gash on his finger hadn't yet closed, and the bandage he wore was now falling off. He found a clean grease rag to wrap around it to keep the blood from dripping.

The office in the station was cold and Brian hurried to light the gas heater. The makeshift safe was actually a hiding place in the tire and tube room at the back of the station, under a pile of used inner tubes. Brian found the cash tray where Orlen had left it the night before and placed it inside the cash register. He switched on the pump lights and opened the service bay door. He rolled out the small washing machine, with its attached hand-cranked wringer and tub filled with icy-cold soapy water, and placed it at the east end of the pump island. He placed a rack of Standard Oil cans on the west end. Once he pulled the used tire rack out for display next to the service bay, he went back inside the office to sit next to the heater. He had no Standard uniform like Orlen did. The only way to distinguish him from a customer was by the orange grease rag that dangled from his back pocket. He normally wore a white t-shirt and Levi's and the one pair of shoes he owned. On cold days he'd wear an extra pair of socks and his letterman's jacket.

He couldn't remember ever being so tired. When he could no longer bear the gnawing dryness in his stomach, he found the keys to the candy dispenser and pop machine and helped himself to a Pepsi and a Salted Nut Roll. From the front window, he could see across Park Street to the railroad tracks. Behind a row of boxcars, he saw the north-side hill and the crudely arranged letter "B" where the "P" once was. He glanced at the wall phone but realized it was still too early to call Deanie.

There wasn't much business between six and eight and Brian sat in the wooden chair with his feet propped up on the desk, trying to get warm and fighting off sleep. A switch engine was busy in the freight yard and Brian heard the occasional crash of coupling boxcars, sometimes jarring him awake.

Orlen had several bulk deliveries and probably wouldn't get back before six that night. Brian reread Orlen's note and looked forward to working on the madam's gold Chrysler as the day warmed up. Around seven, a scruffy-looking hobo suddenly appeared at the office door, holding an empty wine bottle. He startled Brian so bad, Brian almost toppled backward in the chair.

"What do you want?" Brian snapped.

The hobo lifted up his bottle. "Water."

Regaining his composure, Brian pointed to the service bay, telling the man to get his water from the faucet out there.

A few minutes after eight, Joe Parker drove up to the pumps in his dirty blue GMC stock truck, setting off the bell in the back room and jolting Brian awake. Joe was a lifelong resident of Park County, operating a small cattle ranch in Paradise Valley. He wasted no time stepping down from the truck. The sky was clear, but the wind was blowing dust and leaves so hard it looked like someone was cleaning Park Street with a sand blaster.

"Morning," Joe said. His hair was all gray, and a trickle of dark brown spittle dribbled from the corners of his mouth. He wore a long-sleeved checkered shirt and muddy overshoes. "Orlen around?"

"He's out on deliveries, Mr. Parker," Brian said. "Need to see him?"

"Guess not," Joe said. "Just wanted to visit. Fill her up with regular, will you?"

"Brian watched him walk around his truck, kicking the tires."

"By the way," he said, "that was one hell of a game last night. Thought you boys might win the damn thing."

Brian spun the pump crank and reached for the muddy gas cap. The truck was plastered with mud, and splatters of dried manure caked the side rails. An aging Black Angus bull stood motionless in the truck bed.

"Where're you taking your bull, Mr. Parker?"

"To the damn slaughterhouse," Joe answered quickly. "He can't cut it anymore. I put him out there with all those young heifers and all he does is sniff 'em. One time, he had a perpetual hard-on, just like you young guys. Now he can't get it up any better than I can."

Brian laughed. "Sorry to hear that, Mr. Parker."

He finished filling the tank and reached in the cold wash water for the chamois and bug scratcher. From inside the cab, he reached around the window and began the difficult task of cleaning the mud-splattered windshield.

"Well, I'll be damned," Joe said, suddenly noticing the change up on the north-side hill. "You know, in my day, we'd never let Bozeman get away with crap like that."

Brian smiled. "Oh, we got even, Mr. Parker," he said.

"Well, that's good. Say, Brian, isn't this your last year at Park High?"

"Yes, it is," Brian answered. He opened the hood to check the oil.

"What you going to do, then?"

"I haven't any idea," Brian said. "Maybe the railroad or the Army will take me."

Joe shook his head. "Not much opportunity for young folks coming out of high school. This is a beautiful area to live in, but you can't eat the scenery. It's probably best to get the hell out of here. I wouldn't live in this town. You can't trust anyone."

Brian finished up checking under the hood. Listening to Joe opine about life wasn't making his day go any smoother.

"Hell," Joe continued, "all they do around here is steal from each other, usually wives and garbage can lids. But people are probably the same everywhere else," he prattled on. "That's why I live out there at the ranch, by myself."

When Joe finally stepped back up into his truck to drive away, Brian was feeling depressed.

By ten o'clock, the traffic along Park Street had increased and the station was getting busy. Brian wondered if he would ever get started on Charlotte Burk's Chrysler. KPRK was already reporting on the vandalism in Livingston and Bozeman, and Brian surmised that people were out and about to check out the north-side hill for themselves.

Brian's mother drove in just as the noon whistle blew. She had a lunch for Brian and placed the hot plate on the desk in the office. She waited for Brian to make one of his many trips into the office. She looked tired but still pretty.

"Hi, Mom," Brian said, rushing inside. "Need an extra job?"

"Were you involved in this mess in Bozeman last night?" she asked, her voice hurried.

Brian hated to cause her trouble. Life had been hard enough. Raising a child without a husband must have been difficult, especially when she was only a teenager herself. "I'm sorry, Mom," he said, counting out change. "I was there, along with about half the students from Park High."

"Please stay out of trouble, Brian. We don't need any more problems."

Outside, two more cars had lined up for gas. Brian shoved the till shut and rushed out to the pumps. He hoped she'd stay a while, but when he looked again, she was driving away.

Maybe we can talk tonight, he thought.

Business was brisk all day, and it seemed that the island bell never stopped ringing. Customers were demanding every service imaginable, including lubes and tire repairs. Brian had no idea how he was going to handle it all.

At two o'clock, a wonderful thing happened: Dick showed up. Brian was busy pumping gas when he looked up to see Dick limping across I Street. He smiled and waved at Brian as he stepped up to the office door. He had helped out at the station before and was quick to size up the situation. He grabbed a clean grease rag from inside and shoved it in his back pocket.

"Came by to work on the madam's car," Dick said, grinning.

"You're a lifesaver."

At four-thirty, the whistle blew at the shops and Brian was glad the workday was winding down. He wanted to call Deanie all day, but there just wasn't any time. He hoped she would stop by.

It was after five when they finally had time to work on Charlotte Burk's car.

"Let me drive it in on the hoist," Dick said. "There's something sexy about the tan leather seats and the new-car smell."

Brian handed off the keys to Dick. "Go ahead, drive it in. Just watch out for the pecker tracks."

Chapter Thirteen

Orlen got back to the station at a quarter to six. He was a tall, lean man in his fifties. His face was tan with prominent creases. He was still agile with strong arms and hands. He wore a green jacket over his navy-blue Standard Oil work shirt. The sun had begun to set. The wind had calmed some, but the air felt biting cold.

"Feels like winter," Orlen said, stepping into the front office, rubbing his hands.

Brian was closing the overhead door to the service bay, and Dick was wiping down the inside of Charlotte Burk's Chrysler with a chamois.

"I'm sure glad to see you," Brian said, smiling. "This place has been a zoo."

"Looks like you got the madam's car done."

"Yeah, finally. If Dick hadn't come along, I'd still be trying to get to it."

Orlen looked out at the highway. "It looks like things have slowed now. Since Dick's here, why don't the two of you leave a bit early and deliver the Chrysler?"

"You mean you don't want to see the cathouse yourself?" Brian asked, surprised.

"Not really," Orlen shrugged. "I've seen my share of cathouses. Besides, I've got some paperwork to do."

Brian got excited and hollered at Dick to back the Chrysler out to the pumps and fill it with premium. "And," Brian continued, "you and I get to deliver this thing personally to Charlotte."

Both Orlen and Brian laughed when they heard Dick let out a war whoop.

After the Chrysler was filled up, Brian handed Dick the keys to his Chevy. "Sorry, buddy," he said. "I'd better drive the Chrysler."

Just before they pulled away from the station, Orlen stopped them to say, "By the way, good game last night. I almost went out on the field to help out when the fight started."

Brian's eyes were dry and the glare of oncoming headlights made them sting. He felt exhausted, but he enjoyed driving the new car, marveling at how smoothly it took the bumps. He wondered if he'd ever own a car like that.

It was a strange feeling driving into the whorehouse parking lot. Before, just driving by seemed risqué enough. Now, although he was there on business, he still felt that way. The pink porch light was on. There were only a couple of cars in the lot, but when he neared the house, he was surprised by the sight of the mysterious red Pontiac with its California license plates parked close to the back door. Brian parked the Chrysler beside it. Before he stepped on the back porch, he stopped and waited for Dick.

"Hey, this is that California dude's car," Dick said, as he ran up to Brian. "All our local girls must have turned him down," he said, smiling.

While they stood on the porch, Brian didn't know what to expect. He felt nervous and Dick looked as though he might piss his pants. Brian rapped on the screen door and a pretty young woman opened it.

"Hello," she said, her voice soft and pleasant.

She had short light brown hair and worn jeans and a loose-fitting blouse. Somehow she didn't look like what Brian imagined a whore to look like. She didn't look much older than Deanie. With the door open, they looked into the kitchen area. Two other girls were sitting at a table, wearing robes with their hair in curlers. One was reading a magazine, the other filing her nails. Brian surmised that they hadn't yet gotten ready for the evening.

"Can I help you?" the girl asked, smiling.

Brian pointed out at the Chrysler. "I'm from the Standard station," he said. "We've got Charlotte Burk's car serviced."

"Okay, come on in," she said. "I'll get Charlotte."

Inside, the air felt warm and saturated with a heavy flowery scent. They watched the girl walk down a dimly lit hallway and vanish into a misty pink light, adding a hint of mystery to the already erotic atmosphere. The two girls at the table looked up and smiled.

Charlotte was gorgeous—Marilyn Monroe gorgeous. Her face was aglow in dazzling makeup with bright red lipstick. She was tall and slender with long wavy blonde hair. She wore a clinging white dress, cut high on her thighs, revealing most of her well-formed legs. Brian and Dick couldn't help but gawk.

"Hi," she said, smiling, her white teeth sparkling.

Brian felt self-conscious. He still had a bloody grease rag wrapped around his finger, his Levi's were oil stained, and his letterman's jacket still reeked from the fire in Bozeman. He tried to clean his hands, but there were still grease stains around his nails.

"I'm Brian from the Standard station," he said, handing the invoice to Charlotte. He tried not to stare, but he couldn't help it. "This is my helper, Dick. We got your car all serviced."

"Why, thank you. Nice of you to bring it by."

Brian noticed a subtle flare at her nostrils.

She quickly added, "Gosh, I love the smell of the hand cleaner you station fellas use." She escorted them to the table and introduced the girls. "Have a seat. I'll get my checkbook."

Sitting at the table, Brian couldn't believe he was actually in a whorehouse. He kept having this feeling like he was somehow breaking the law. Yet sitting there was like being in a typical family kitchen, with bowls of leftovers on the table and dirty dishes stacked in the sink. The only giveaway, perhaps, was that the two girls in robes weren't wearing much of anything underneath. They didn't bother to keep their robes closed, nor did they seem to care that Brian and Dick could easily see their bare breasts. Dick started a conversation with a girl named Marianne.

"I met Orlen," Charlotte said, handing her check to Brian. "Never saw you two before."

"I only work part time, ma'am. Dick helps me once in a while."

"Oh, please, don't call me ma'am. Sounds like I'm an old lady."

Brian smiled and said he was sorry.

She took Brian's hand. "You just call me Char, okay?"

They walked over to the door and Charlotte opened it. Suddenly, Brian felt Dick jab him in the ribs, prodding Brian to ask Charlotte the big question.

Brian paused in the doorway. "I have to ask," he said, turning to Charlotte. "Could we come out sometime?" He felt himself blushing.

Charlotte smiled. "I'm going to surprise you, Brian. I get that question a lot from younger men. The fact is the sheriff keeps his eye on this place, and he doesn't want any irate mothers calling him complaining about their boys being introduced to new vices. But, having said that, my answer is, maybe."

Dick's eyes lit up.

"My girls would love to entertain you," she went on. "But not tonight. Saturdays are just too busy. Try the weeknights, and for heaven's sake, don't tell your moms."

"Yahoo!" Dick bellowed as they climbed into Brian's Chevy. He seemed to be in a trance. The smile wouldn't leave his face. "Did you see those tits?"

Brian started the Chevy and headed back to town. It was exciting, but oddly, he didn't feel as sexually charged as Dick did. His thoughts about sex were with Deanie. As they drove, Dick continued to ramble on about Marianne and how he couldn't wait to get in the sack with her. Brian couldn't get his mind off why Deanie hadn't called him all day.

Chapter Fourteen

Deanie stayed in her room most of the day Saturday. She passed up breakfast and wouldn't take any phone calls. It wasn't until she declined lunch that her mother decided to pay her a visit.

"You feeling all right, Deanie?" her mother asked.

Deanie sat up in her bed, resting her head against the headboard. She felt terrible. Her stomach still hurt. Her mother opened the shades and rays of sunlight beamed in. Her mother's familiar cologne brought freshness into the room. Still youthful, her mother wore a pretty blue dress. She sat on the bed and brushed Deanie's hair from her face.

"Why won't you take any calls?" she asked. "All the Belles have called, Karen three times. What's wrong?"

Deanie burst into tears and reached for her mother's hand. "Oh, Mom," she cried. "Guys are awful." She wanted to blurt out what Bill did to her, but then she remembered what happened with Brian and thought it best not to tell.

Karen came over to the house around three. She was quick to scold Deanie about not taking calls. She made Deanie get dressed and insisted she get out of the house. Deanie tossed on her jeans and a sweatshirt. She didn't bother with makeup, merely running a brush through her hair and donning a scarf. Karen had her mother's black Buick. The heater made whirring noises, but the warmth felt good and Karen left it on.

"I've been worried sick about you, Deanie," Karen said, backing out of the driveway. "You okay?"

Deanie shrugged. "I guess so."

"You don't sound very convincing," Karen said. "Last night was wild."

"What do you mean wild?"

Karen looked at Deanie, surprised. "What, what do you mean, what do I mean? Are you kidding? I'm talking about you and Bill, Brian and Dick, the raid on Bozeman, our big drunk, all of it."

"I guess I haven't gotten all the news yet, Karen. What about Brian?"

"Well, the good news is he isn't in jail. Some Bozeman guys changed our 'P' into a 'B' last night. In retaliation, a bunch of Park High kids raided Bozeman's football field and set it on fire. Brian and Dick were in on it."

"Wow! So what's the bad news?"

"I went by the station on the way over here. Brian's working, but he looks like his butt's dragging. Dick's there helping him. Want to swing by there?"

"No," Deanie answered quickly. "I can't see him right now."

Karen drove toward downtown and they looked at the vandalism on the hill. On the south end of Livingston, Karen pulled into the root beer stand.

"I think it's time you told me about you and Bill, Deanie."

Deanie began to cry. "I always thought of myself as a good girl, Karen. Now I'm not so sure."

Karen ordered two regulars from the young carhop. "You are a good girl, Deanie."

"I wonder. In the span of two nights, I've been made by two different guys."

"You mean, you and Bill did it?"

"At first, I thought I was being raped," Deanie cried. "But after it was over, I realized I didn't fight hard enough. I just gave up and let him do it. I feel so ashamed of myself."

"Bill sure has changed," Karen said. "I used to think he was a nice guy."

"He's just like all guys," Deanie said. "They only have one thing on their minds."

The root beer was ice cold and Karen took quick sips. Deanie held the frosted mug against her forehead, hoping to soothe her headache.

"We spent a lot of time searching for you," Karen said. "We got so drunk, we plotted all kinds of revenge against Bill, from wrecking his car to castrating him. We drove up on the Point, looking for Brian and Dick. We were going to tell Brian that you were kidnapped and let him take care of Bill himself. When we got up there, everyone had left, leaving a perfectly warm bonfire going to waste. We sent Linda back to see her brother for more vodka. We stayed up there and got totally smashed."

Deanie took a few sips of the root beer and handed the mug to Karen to place on the window tray. She slumped down in the seat. "What am I going to do about Brian?"

Karen finished her drink and tapped lightly on the horn. The carhop came and retrieved the tray.

"If you love Brian, don't do anything," she said, driving away from the stand. "Spare both of you any more grief. Never tell Brian about Bill."

"I'm sure Bill won't leave me alone for sure now," Deanie said.

"There's a big fight brewing, isn't there?"

"Oh, God," Deanie groaned. "There probably will be, if Brian finds out about Bill."

Karen drove south along the river, making a loop around Sacagawea Park. A few mallards were bobbing among the cattails at one end of the lagoon. Crystals of ice were already forming along the shore. Karen parked along the hedge next to the football field. The field wasn't green anymore. Much of the browning grass was trampled or worn away. The wind had almost completely stripped the leaves from the cottonwoods, and they now piled up around the bleachers. Deanie wondered how differently things might be if she had gone with Brian after the dance.

"You won't believe what happened next," Karen said. "Linda went crazy when she discovered that she could see the pink porch light of the whorehouse from up on the Point. She got this bright idea that she was going to go knock on the front door and ask to see her brother, Greg."

Deanie laughed.

"Sometimes I worry about that girl," Karen continued. "So, Colleen loads us all in the car and we drive over there, right up to the front porch. Linda didn't even flinch and stomped up to the porch. We were all laughing our butts off."

"That's our Linda."

"She rapped on the screen door and stood there with her hands on her hips, cock sure of herself. This beautiful blonde came to the door, and Linda talked with her a minute before the blonde slammed the door in her face."

"What did Linda say to her?"

"We couldn't hear, but it wouldn't be beyond her to have asked the lady for a job."

In the distance, they heard the shop's whistle.

"I'd better get my mom's car back," Karen said. She turned the car around and headed east.

"How do you do it, Karen?"

"What do you mean?"

"How do you keep from going all the way?"

Karen smiled. "I don't know. It's really tough with Dick. He wants it so badly."

When Karen pulled up in front of Deanie's house, Deanie's mother was out under the clothesline, struggling in the wind to hang out wet sheets.

"Sometimes it isn't the guys that worry me," Deanie said. "Sometimes it's me."

"Try not to be so hard on yourself, Deanie. We're only human."

"I know, but aren't we supposed to be virgins when we get married?"

Karen shrugged. "I think it's a big myth. Being a virgin at marriage might be the exception. Anyway, what happened, happened. Let it be."

Deanie wiped the tears from her eyes. "But you're a virgin, Karen."

"Yes, but I don't necessarily want to be."

Deanie opened the car door. "Thanks for being there, Karen. I'd better go help Mom before the wind blows her away."

Chapter Fifteen

By the next Monday morning, six inches of snow had accumulated in Livingston. Orlen Picard had predicted snow on Sunday morning when he stepped out of the station's office and looked up at the gray sky. "Get ready for winter," he had said. "When the air is cold and the wind dies down, watch out. Besides that, Monday is Halloween; we always get snow by Halloween."

Brian hated snow, especially when he had to work in it. It started snowing Sunday afternoon, causing a brisk business with customers in a panic to get snow tires on their vehicles, and whenever Brian found time, he shoveled snow away from the gas pumps. Now, getting ready for school, he dreaded going out in it again. He wished he would have invested in some overshoes. He managed to wrap a new bandage on his finger, wondering if he should go and get stitches in it. He was nervous about seeing Deanie at school. She hadn't called all weekend.

He used his mother's broom to sweep off his car. When he started it, he wondered if his balding tires had enough traction to get through the snow. It had quit snowing during the night, but the flakes flying off the hood made it necessary to keep the windshield wipers going. The heater had barely warmed the car before Brian got to Dick's house. Dick was waiting on his front steps. He had already made up a few snowballs, and as soon as Brian was within range, he began pelting the Chevy.

"Well, this is my big day," Dick said, sliding inside the car.

Brian laughed. "Going trick-or-treating?"

"Yup, I'm going out to the cathouse to see Marianne."

"Thought you had basketball practice today," Brian said.

"I mean after that."

"Looks like you're still limping. How's the leg?"

"Hurts like hell," Dick said. "I think it's more swollen than ever. Been popping aspirin like jellybeans."

48

Even though they arrived early, Brian still couldn't find a parking place. He had to park a half-block down the street. When the three-story building was built in 1929, apparently no one thought a parking lot was necessary.

The school was abuzz with chatter about the raid on Bozeman's field. Some thought of it as the best Halloween trick of all times. Brian and Dick were surrounded with well-wishers the moment they walked into the school; a few even congratulated them on the game. Brian's one class he shared with Deanie wasn't until later in the afternoon, but he hoped he'd see her in the halls.

Brian's first class was American History. He spent most of the hour writing a note to Deanie, telling her about the events over the last three days. He told her he loved and missed her and hoped she would come by the station that afternoon. While he wrote, the loudspeaker switched on, informing the entire school there was to be a general assembly the second period. Brian saw Karen and a couple other Belles in the hallways but didn't see Deanie. He gave his note to Karen to give to Deanie. It wasn't until he got seated in the auditorium that he spotted her several rows away. She looked beautiful in a navy-blue skirt and white blouse. She didn't turn to wave at him.

The principal, Mr. Short, looked angry as he walked briskly up onto the stage, carrying a folded newspaper in his hand. Strolling a few steps behind him was Park County Sheriff McCarthy, holding his white Stetson hat and looking all business. He wore neatly pressed tanned shirt and slacks. His large caliber revolver bulged out from his belt.

"Have any of you seen this newspaper?" Mr. Short began.

He unfolded the *Bozeman Daily Chronicle* and held it high over his head, causing an immediate roar of laughter and whistling. On the front cover were pictures of the disfigured "P" on Livingston's north-side hill and the Hawks' football field. An ambitious photographer had somehow positioned himself atop one of Hawks' goalpost crossbeams and snapped a picture of the entire football field. Much of the grass had been scorched, but to the credit of Dan Buckley, a perfect letter "P" had been emblazoned in the middle of the field.

Mr. Short brought the paper quickly to his side and motioned for the clamor to stop. "This is serious business!" he shouted. "We know that some of you students participated in this vandalism, and we will not tolerate this kind of behavior. Further, there was beer confiscated that night and the authorities are investigating." He then turned to the sheriff. "Sheriff McCarthy is here to find out who brought the beer. Anyone with information can come to my office after the assembly and talk with him."

By the time Brian made it to his next class—PE—he was anxious to talk to Dick. He met up with him in the hall just before he got to the gym.

"No sense worrying about the beer," Dick shrugged. "They can't tag us with it. I think Buckley should be a little nervous, though."

"What if they got a description of my car?"

"Well, they didn't catch us with it, did they? Stop worrying."

When they entered the doors to the gym, Brian was surprised to see Dan Buckley and Ray Hudson talking with everyone who entered.

"You two keep your mouth shut about the beer," Buckley told them in a low voice. "I'm on probation and if I get nailed for the beer, they'll send me up."

Coach LeClaire ran PE class and was standing next to the thick rope that dangled from the rafters. Just before it was Brian's turn to compete in the rope climbing event, the coach looked at the bloody bandage on his finger. He then turned to examine Dick's leg.

"Looks like you two got the worst of it in the last football game," the coach said. "I'm issuing the both of you a pass to go over to the Park Clinic and get checked out."

Chapter Sixteen

Deanie felt terrible about avoiding Brian. She missed him, but she didn't know how she was going to hide her guilt when she saw him again. It wasn't until she read Brian's note that she felt she had the courage to face him. She hoped Karen was right, and if she never brought it up, perhaps she and Brian would be okay.

Deanie talked with each of the Belles during the day but managed to avoid giving them any lengthy discussions as to what happened with Bill. She could only give Karen the details. There was no cheerleading practice that afternoon, and Deanie looked forward to going home when her last class ended. She had just opened her locker when Linda rushed up to her.

"I hate Mr. Cline's English class," Linda said, a little out of breath from running. "Tommy Anderson sits behind me. One time he actually reached under the seat and pinched my butt. Today, he wanted to know what color panties I had on, wanted me to pull up my skirt to show him."

Deanie couldn't help but laugh. "Well, did you show him?"

"No, but I thought about it," she answered, grinning.

Deanie rearranged her books and grabbed her coat and scarf. She hoped she could get away from Linda before the heavy questions started, but before she could lose her in the crowd, Linda called out, "Can you give me a ride home?"

Outside, the wind blew hard and cold against Deanie's face. She pulled her scarf across her cheeks and turned her head away from the wind. They didn't try to talk until they reached Deanie's Chevy. A new Dodge pickup with a full gun rack mounted in the back window was parked behind Deanie, and they noticed a dead bull elk lying in the pickup bed. Deanie and Linda were about to step inside Deanie's Car when Bill Slater called out from the idling pickup.

"Hey, girls, jump in my uncle's truck, where it's warm."

Deanie was startled and hurried inside her car. Linda paused for a moment, holding the door open, gawking back at Bill.

"I'm not going anywhere with him, Linda," Deanie said, starting the car. "Either get in or go with him."

Linda finally got inside. The windows frosted over quickly, and Deanie scraped at them with her fingernails. She was about to turn out into the street even without clear vision when Bill suddenly burst open the passenger door, nudging Linda over enough to sit down. He was wearing hunting packs, wool pants, and a shirt. He smelled of smoke and pine needles.

"So what do you think of my elk?" Bill asked, smiling.

"He looks like a beautiful animal," Linda said.

"Thanks. I got him up the Boulder this morning."

"You should be glad," Linda said. "Sometimes my dad and brothers go the whole hunting season without even seeing an elk."

It frustrated Deanie that the heater took so long to warm up. "I have to get going, Bill," she snapped.

"Okay," Bill said. "I just wanted you to know that once I get my cow tag filled, I'm leaving for home. I won't be back 'til spring. I thought you might like to see me again before I leave."

"I don't think so, Bill," Deanie said.

Bill stretched across Linda in an attempt to steal a kiss from Deanie, but Deanie moved her head away. As soon as Bill was out of the car, Deanie threw the Chevy into gear, but the tires merely spun in the snow. Bill had ample time to get back into his truck and outmaneuver her. He swerved out into the street ahead of her, waving as he passed by.

Chapter Seventeen

It was three-thirty when Brian and Dick finally left the clinic. The doctor put five stitches in Brian's finger to get the rip closed. They found a fracture in Dick's left fibula. It took most of the day getting him processed. When it was over, Dick was sporting a cast up to his knee. The nurse had to cut open his pant leg, all the way to his hip, in order for his pants to fit over the cast. The clinic loaned him a pair of crutches, which he battled to get the hang of. The overcast sky was already showing signs of darkness when Brian pulled up to Dick's house.

"This cast could screw up my sex life," Dick said, struggling out of the car.

"I know," Brian said. "Say nothing about your basketball career."

"Why don't you come over and get me after work? Maybe we can go out to the cathouse."

Brian smiled and waved. "I'll see."

The four-o'clock whistle blew just as Brian pulled into the station. The outside lights were on, and Orlen was shoveling snow away from the pumps. Brian hoped it wouldn't snow any more that day. Staying inside and cleaning up was much more appealing. A little after five, Brian had just started hosing down the floor of the service bay when the bell rang again. He dreaded going back outside, but when he saw that it was Deanie's white Chevy, he excitedly raced outside. He leaped in the passenger side and wrapped his arms tightly around Deanie.

"God, I've missed you, Deanie."

Deanie had tears in her eyes. "I'm sorry, Brian. I don't want to be away from you anymore."

"My life is a total mess without you, Deanie." Brian kissed her on the mouth and held her.

They were quiet for a time, only clinging to each other, kissing.

Finally, Brian asked, "Did you see this old boyfriend of yours again the other night?"

Deanie hesitated before answering. "Yes, just for a short while. He sort of corralled me."

Brian's mind raced with fearful suspicion. "Did anything happen, Deanie?"

Deanie tried to turn away, but Brian held her firmly. Finally, she looked at him and lied. "I kissed him once, Brian. He wanted a kiss goodbye."

Suddenly, a gas customer pulled up on the other side of the island. He not only wanted gas but wanted Brian to check under the hood, unconcerned that it was cold and dark or that Brian's mind was totally engaged elsewhere. Worried that Deanie might leave, Brian worked as fast as he could. He felt relieved when he finally finished up, but he was soon disappointed to see another customer pull in. It was a hunter with an elk in his pickup.

"Nice bull," Brian said as politely as he could.

"You must be Brian West," the guy said. A ribbon of smoke swirled out of the cab.

"That's me," Brian said. "Do I know you?"

"Ask Deanie who I am."

Brian's heart quickened and fear surged through him. He knew who the guy was. "You're the dude from California, aren't you?"

"Yup," he said, offering to shake hands. "The name's Bill Slater."

Brian ignored his hand and leaned against the door panel. "So, what do you want?"

"Not very friendly, are you?" Bill said with a smirk on his face.

"I'll ask you once more, pal. What do you want?"

"Just one thing," Bill said. "Deanie."

Brian clinched his fist and fought back the urge to reach inside for Bill's throat. "Well, I don't think Deanie wants you."

Deanie had her window rolled up and her back to them. When Brian tapped on the window, Deanie lowered it slowly.

"Tell this guy to get lost, Deanie."

Her eyes were filled with tears. All she did was mouth the words "I love you."

"Then, tell him, Deanie."

Deanie sat staring out at him, her eyes wide with fear.

"Deanie, tell him," Brian pleaded.

Finally, Deanie moved the shift lever. "I have to go home," she said, tears streaming down her cheeks.

"Either you tell him or it's over between us, Deanie."

Brian watched in disbelief as Deanie rolled up the window and pulled away from the pumps. When he heard a chuckle coming from the pickup, he lunged for the window of the cab. Bill tried to lock the door and roll up the window at the same time. He did manage to get the door locked, but the window was down just far enough to allow Brian's fist to smack the left side of his head. Brian reached for the door lock, but Bill had the pickup in gear and he stomped down on the gas pedal. Brian gave chase, but the pickup fishtailed through the snow and sped off down Park Street.

Chapter Eighteen

Livingston's winds were usually so ferocious and constant that the snow seldom stayed long on the ground. Piles of snow would gather in drifts, like sand dunes, leaving much of the yellowing landscape bare. By mid-December, several snowstorms had come and gone, but little snow had accumulated on the yards and streets. No one had reassembled the "P" on the north-side hill, but drifting snow had obliterated the letter "B."

Brian stayed true to his threat in breaking up with Deanie. He hadn't talked to her in over a month. He was a long way from being over her, and it pained him to see her at school each day, reminding him how beautiful she was, knowing she could never be his. Whenever she came near, he hated the role he had to play, pretending she didn't matter anymore. The nights were the worst when he was alone. He seldom got to talk with his mother. She continued to work odd shifts at the truck stop.

Like most residents of Livingston, Brian disliked winter. While some skied at Bridger Bowl, a few miles to the west, Brian considered winter a season of cold and misery that had to be endured, not enjoyed. He tried to stay out of the weather as much as he could, but during Christmas vacation, he and Dick decided to go out looking for Christmas trees. Brian borrowed an ax from Orlen, and the two of them drove the Chevy up Mill Creek, south of town. Dick had helped himself to two six-packs of his dad's stash of Great Falls Select, thinking he'd never miss them. His dad bought beer a truckload at a time. Since his back injury, he stopped working at the shops and now lay around the house all day, drinking beer.

The sky that day was clear and painted a pale blue. Dick was still in his cast but an expert in getting around on one good foot, with or without his crutches; however, the cast was well beaten up and dirty. It was becoming obvious that he wouldn't be able to get back out on the basketball court. The doctor didn't like the way Dick's leg was healing and had told Dick that the cast had to stay on for a while longer. Oddly, Dick didn't seem to mind. He had his first sexual experience at the whorehouse shortly after he got the cast. Despite his fears, the cast never posed a problem.

"I just drop the cast off to one side of her, out of the way, and plop the rest of me between her legs," Dick said, grinning. "It doesn't bother me a bit."

Because Charlotte had allowed Dick in the whorehouse during weekdays, he was having the time of his life with Marianne. He made up a story for his parents that he had a part-time job so that his dad would let him use his pickup. After school, he'd drive out to the whorehouse and stay until around ten every night. Charlotte didn't mind him being there as long as he paid for the services. Dick managed to scrounge enough money from relatives and friends, including Brian. Charlotte even allowed Dick to drink beer if he brought his own. Brian only got to see him when his dad's pickup needed gas. When Karen began to ask Brian about Dick, Brian backed up Dick's ruse about the part-time job.

The beer went down easily as they drove over the graveled road. It was fun being around Dick. Somehow he had a knack for getting Brian out of his gloomy moods. It was always that way, ever since that summer between their fifth and sixth grades, when Dick peddled his bicycle along the sidewalk in front of Brian's house, stopping to gawk at Brian working on his own bike in the front yard of the rented house he and his mother lived in. Brian had his bike upside down, struggling to replace the chain that had slipped off the sprocket. Dick surprised him when he hollered over at him, "Do ya wanna race?"

Brian looked up quickly and stared out at Dick's confident, freckled face. Dick wasn't smiling and Brian wasn't sure how to react to him.

"I wouldn't race anyone with this piece of crap," he said. "Both tires are flat and the handlebars are about to fall off."

"Oh, I don't mean bike racing," Dick said quickly. "I'm talking foot racing."

"Boy, you sure are cocky. You think you're fast or something?"

"Well," Dick said, smiling. "We just moved here from Staples, Minnesota. I was the fastest kid in town there. I want to see how I do against kids here."

"I'm pretty fast myself," Brian said, trying hard not to be intimidated.

Dick laid his bike down across the sidewalk. "I'll race you to the corner."

Brian didn't want to race the brash kid, but he also couldn't back down from the challenge. "Sure, why not?" The corner looked to be about one hundred yards.

They positioned their high-top black canvas shoes on one of the cracks in the sidewalk, and on Dick's count to three, they tore off for the corner. Dick was ahead right from the start. Brian ran his hardest, but Dick beat him to the corner by at least four strides.

Panting, they walked back to Brian's yard.

"Don't feel bad," Dick said. "You really are fast. My mom thinks I was born with rubber in my legs."

"You beat me fair and square," Brian said. "You just might be the fastest kid in this town, too."

Before Dick picked up his bicycle from the sidewalk, he walked over to look at Brian's bike. "Can you get this thing running again?"

Brian lifted the bike back on the tires. "Most of it," he said. "But the handlebars got bent so bad that the metal has cracked and is about to break in two."

"You know what?" Dick said after thinking about the problem for a moment. "I think I know where to find some bars that'll fit this bike."

"Really?"

"Yeah, I think so. I'll be back tomorrow. Maybe we can go riding together."

The next morning, Dick showed up with a shiny set of handlebars, equipped with red rubber hand grips. Dick helped remove the old bars and install the new ones. Brian felt so thrilled, he forgot to even ask where Dick got them. He often wondered about them, but after a time, he just accepted them as a gift. That was the beginning of their friendship.

Now, as Brian drove up Mill Creek, feeling the beer, he thought again about those handlebars and wondered anew where Dick had gotten them.

A few miles before they started to ascend into the mountains where the trees were, they noticed an old abandoned Hudson sitting just off the highway on a steep hillside that sloped toward the creek. Its wheels and motor were gone and its hood lay off to one side. The hillside was covered with drifted snow, and both of them had had enough beer to think it would be fun to slide down it on their butts. They parked off the side of the highway and clamored up the hill. Brian pulled the rusted hood from the snow and thought it would make a great toboggan. Without hesitation, Brian flipped the hood upside down, and with one hand holding a beer, the other hanging onto the sharp edges of the hood, they shoved off down the steep slope, Brian up front and Dick in the back. The hood tore down the slope, banging into unseen boulders just beneath the snow. They soon realized that both hands were needed to hang on, and the beer cans were quickly discarded. Three quarters of the way down, Dick flipped out. His casted leg smashed against a rock, and he tumbled all the way to the bottom. Brian managed to stay aboard until the hood smacked into the level ground and toppled over. Brian landed a few feet beyond the hood. Both of them were laughing, although Dick was clutching his bad leg. Both of them had cut their palms on the sharp edges of the hood, and Dick had crushed in one side of his cast.

The snow covering Mill Creek Road had been packed down enough that Brian's Chevy made it all the way up East Fork, where the pine trees became more accessible from the road. Brian stopped when they spotted some Christmas tree prospects, and he decided to trudge up the mountain with the ax in hand. From the road, Dick was to guide Brian to the good trees. Brian thought he had found a bushy fir not far from the road, but Dick pointed for Brian to look farther up the slope at a forty-foot lodge pole.

"The top of that tree would make the perfect Christmas tree," Dick said.

"You're kidding," Brian said, looking skyward.

"Chop it down," Dick insisted. "If you're going to wimp out, I'll come up there and do it myself."

"You're crazy," Brian said, shaking his head. "Anything for a friend, right?" Brian said, plowing ahead. When he reached the tree, he called down to Dick, "This one?"

"That's it. Get chopping, old buddy."

The trunk was thick, but Orlen's ax was sharp. When Brian had chopped through most of the tree trunk, it dawned on him that the tree could actually reach the Chevy below him when it fell. Dick must have had the same concern, and before the lodge pole began to tip, he hurriedly started the car and moved it a few yards forward. Brian was amazed that the top of the tree fell at the exact spot where the car had been parked.

"You'd make a lousy logger," Dick said.

It was late in the afternoon when they finished topping the Christmas tree from the lodge pole. Brian hurried back to where the small fir was and chopped it down, too. Once they had the trees loaded on top of the car, they headed back to town, laughing and enjoying the beer.

Chapter Nineteen

The winter winds blasted Livingston so hard, Brian was amazed the houses could withstand such force. At night, cold air whistled in through the broken pane in Brian's bedroom, spraying fine grains of snow across his bed. The whine of the wind made him feel lonesome. He ached to have Deanie back, yet it was equally painful knowing she had been unfaithful. Bill Slater had left Livingston before Brian could have it out with him. It was intolerable to think Slater had gotten away with it. The night of the breakup, Brian drove all over town looking for him. Although he was glad to have landed one good punch, it wasn't satisfying, and as he lay in bed, he envisioned all the ways he would beat Slater if he ever saw him again.

In mid-January, a bad strain of flu hit Livingston. The schools didn't close, but over forty percent of the students went absent. Brian started getting symptoms one weekend while working the station. Headaches and fever forced him into bed, and he stayed away from school a whole week. With his mother working, Brian nursed himself as best he could. He experienced both chills and fever, sometimes becoming delirious, drifting in and out of sleep. He had terrifying nightmares, and often, he wasn't sure if he was awake or dreaming. One afternoon, he opened his eyes to see fading sunlight filtering in through the drawn shades and out across the floor. He saw a figure of a girl standing next to his bed. In the dim light, she looked like Deanie. If he was dreaming, he wanted it to be Deanie. He watched her undress and position herself in the direct sunrays so Brian could see her clearly. It was Deanie, but it wasn't until she drew his covers back and lay next to him that he accepted the fact that he wasn't dreaming. Deanie was actually there, naked and in his bed, just as he so often fantasized.

Chapter Twenty

Shortly before Bill Slater left for California, Deanie was convinced her life was completely out of control and perhaps unsalvageable. At times, she accepted the fact that she and Brian were finished. She thought she no longer deserved him. Even though she loved him, she had hurt him so badly she had no right to try and hold on to him. She hadn't told him the whole truth, but he probably figured it all out anyway.

While Brian stayed away from her, Bill stayed persistent. He called her house so often, Deanie's mother was getting annoyed. Over the phone, he did his best to charm her, telling her how beautiful she was and how the agency he worked for wanted to hire her. The La Belle six all had different opinions on what she should do. Some of them were intrigued with the California job, but Karen warned her to stay clear of Bill Slater.

One day, Bill drove down to her house and parked out in front. He wouldn't leave until Deanie came outside. As she listened to Bill try to convince her to see him again, she came to accept the fact that Brian was no longer in her life. Finally, she agreed to see Bill once more. He invited her over to his uncle's house to taste some wine he had brought back from California. After the wine bottle was empty, Deanie consented to going to bed with him. They continued to do this for the next three days before Bill left for California.

When Bill left, Deanie felt strangely alone and each passing day brought increased feelings of guilt. She hadn't talked much to Karen, and at school, she couldn't bear to look at Brian. His presence in class compounded her anxiety. She decided to go and tell Karen everything, and one afternoon she asked Karen to go for a ride with her. She had hoped that if she confessed all, she might find some relief. As it turned out, Karen was furious with her.

"You're acting like a slut, Deanie!" Karen shouted at her. "You don't love Bill. At least be decent enough to love the guy you're screwing."

Deanie began to cry. She drove up Calendar Street, avoiding Park Street, where Brian might be working. The downtown shops were getting ready to close up, and Deanie circled the drag. KPRK was playing "*This Magic Moment*," by the Drifters.

"Please don't hate me, Karen. I need your friendship more than ever."

Karen made an irritated sigh. "I don't hate you, Deanie. You just make me so damn mad sometimes. Brian is so right for you. He's a sweet and caring guy. He might not have a pot to piss in right now, but someday he will. You're giving him up for a no-good, con-man.."

"Brian doesn't want me. How could he?"

Karen turned quickly to Deanie. "Because he doesn't have to know what you did, damn it! Just stop doing what you've been doing."

"Oh, Karen, I wish I could do it all over. Going all the way became too easy once I broke that first-time barrier. That great taboo doesn't seem to have the same significance now."

There was a hint of fading sunlight in the clear sky as Deanie turned at the corner on Main Street to start back to Karen's house. Fine ribbons of snow blew on the street ahead of the car. The airflow from the heater felt warm at their feet.

"What about you and Dick?" Deanie asked. "Are you still going together?"

"I don't know," Karen answered quickly. "He's acting weird. He says he's got some job in the afternoon now. I seldom see him anymore."

"I'm sorry, Karen. Please don't take this the wrong way, but I'm convinced you'll never keep a guy very long unless you give in to him."

When Deanie pulled up to Karen's house, Karen paused a moment before getting out.

"I'm sure you're right, Deanie," she said. "Right now, I just don't know what to do about it."

Cheerleader practices and basketball games kept Deanie busy throughout the holidays. Some of the games were out of town, and even though he didn't call her anymore, Deanie hated being that much farther away from Brian. The winter roads were treacherous, and she always felt relieved when the bus rolled back into Livingston.

When she didn't get her period in November, she assumed it was because of all the stress she was under. Only after she was more than thirty days late did she dare think the worst. She couldn't imagine being pregnant, but the fear of it made her ill. Soon she stopped going to practices, and after school each day, she confined herself to her room, telling her mother she didn't feel well.

"It's that Asian flu bug," her mother said. "Everyone in town is getting it."

Increasingly, Deanie isolated herself, avoiding everyone, including Karen. She felt too ashamed to face anyone. At night she'd lie in bed, worrying, praying that if she was pregnant, it was by Brian and not Bill Slater. She might not deserve Brian, but she still loved him. Perhaps he would take her back. Perhaps he could one day forgive her.

When she learned he was down with the flu, she felt an urge to go to him. One afternoon, she let herself in the back door of Brian's house and found Brian shivering under a pile of blankets. He looked awfully sick and only partially conscious. Thinking that her body heat might lessen his chills, she undressed and lay beside him. At first he seemed unaware or her presence, but in time, he began to respond to her as she pressed herself against his feverish body. Brian never spoke, but eventually he took her into his arms, pulling her beneath him. They made love, again and again, until Deanie became concerned that Brian's mother might come home.

Chapter Twenty-one

One week in February, arid Chinook winds surged in from the Southwest, warming up much of Montana. Temperatures soared into the fifties, and the snow piles began to melt. Everyone knew the nice weather was short lived, but they took to enjoying it while it lasted, removing their heavy winter coats and donning short-sleeved shirts. Kids frolicked about the playgrounds again, and the trees looked as though they might start budding.

On Saturday afternoon, Deanie brought her Chevy to the station to get it serviced. Brian was delighted to see her there, although she looked completely out of place in those drab and dirty surroundings. She was clean and fresh and wore a light-yellow dress that fit her snugly at her waist and flared out at her hips. Brian carried one of the wooden office chairs out into the service bay so that she could watch him while he changed the oil and greased the joints.

"Don't touch anything," Brian told her while he had the Chevy up on the hoist. "I don't want you to get that pretty dress dirty."

He was glad they were back together again, although it still pained him to think she had cheated on him. He promised her he wouldn't talk about Bill Slater anymore.

When Brian finished with her car, she decided to stay at the station until he closed up. The station's business was brisk that day, and Deanie kept busy scanning through a stack of old *Life* magazines Orlen kept on one of the shelves in the office. When Brian finally got to lock the station up, he drove them out on Willow Creek Road in Deanie's Chevy. The melting snow had made the road muddy and sloppy, but passable. The wind was robust, but the air felt pleasantly warm. The road meandered up a short grade. On top, Brian found a spot to park just off the side of the road, letting Deanie's Chevy idle, keeping the heater on. The night sky was clear, and a partial moon lit up the hills to the north. The radio was working and for a time they snuggled together, enjoying the music. KPRK was playing a series of country western songs and they listened to Jim Reeves, Patsy Cline, and Faron Young. Soon they both undressed and began making love. Deanie was exceptionally affectionate, holding Brian tightly with her arms and legs, not allowing him to pull away. Brian knew it wasn't a good thing to do, but it was very easy to oblige.

When they finished, Deanie continued to cling to him, holding him on top of her. "I love you so much, Brian," she said. "Please never leave me again."

Brian kissed her softly, sensing the fear in her voice. "I won't, Deanie. Are you okay?"

"No," she said quickly, her voice suddenly desperate. "I'm pregnant, Brian."

Stunned, Brian forced himself from her hold and sat up in the seat. He felt dizzy and suddenly nauseated. All he could think of to say was "How do you know?" He reached for his clothes while his mind filled with many more questions.

Deanie began to weep. She rose up but didn't bother to gather her clothes. "I just know, Brian. I figure I'm four months along."

"Four months! My God, Deanie. Why didn't you tell me?"

"I've been so scared, Brian," she sobbed. "I don't want to lose you."

Deanie began to shiver and Brian wrapped his letterman's jacket around her. He pulled her to him, and she cried against his chest. Suddenly, a greater fear soared inside him, even before he was fully conscious of it. He felt a stinging grip at his stomach, neck, and legs. His heart pounded and he began breathing hard.

"Deanie!" he cried out. "Four months ago, Bill Slater was here."

"Oh, God, don't say it, Brian," she lashed out at him, slapping at his chest.

Brian grabbed her arms. She struggled for a moment, and then sobbed against Brian's shoulder.

"Don't, Brian. Please don't."

Brian was torn between consoling her and fighting back his own fears. When she began to calm down some, Brian couldn't hold back any longer. He couldn't help but ask, "Did Slater make you that night, Deanie?"

Deanie pushed away and pressed up against the door. She shouted at him hysterically, "Yes, he made me, Brian. He forced me down in the car seat and he made me. There, I said it."

There was a buzzing sensation deep inside Brian's head, then a sharp, stinging pain. On impulse, he swung at Deanie, hitting her on her left cheekbone.

Her head smacked against the window. When she screamed, Brian cocked his arm to strike again, but thankfully, he regained his senses. He flung open the door and hung his head over the threshold and vomited. When he looked back, Deanie was fleeing from the car, her yellow dress bundled in her arms, her creamy bare skin fading off into the darkness. Clad only in his t-shirt and Levi's, Brian raced after her, both of them barefooted, sloshing through the cold, crusted mud.

Deanie stayed on the road, running as fast as she could toward town. Brian gained on her quickly but gasped in terror when he saw headlight beams approaching in the road ahead. He had to get her under control. What explanation would there be for chasing after a hysterical, bruised, and naked girl down a dark country road?

When he got to within a body length, he made a diving tackle, slamming his shoulder into the back of her legs. Deanie fell forward, and they both skidded to the side of the road through the icy mud.

Deanie screamed at him, "Leave me alone!"

She tried to regain her feet, but Brian held her down. The headlights were nearly up to them.

"I'm sorry I hit you, Deanie," Brian said, desperate to get her calmed down.

As the car came near, Deanie attempted to wave her arms, but Brian grabbed her and rolled with her down into the slight snow-filled barrow pit. He covered her mouth and positioned his body over hers until the car passed, splattering them with slush as it went by. Brian waited until the taillights had faded before letting Deanie loose.

"I hate you!" Deanie screamed, trembling.

Her face was smeared in tears, mascara, and mud, and in the moonlight, Brian saw a puffy bruise just under her eye. He draped her yellow dress around her and scooped her up, swinging her across his shoulders. He raced back up the road to the car, his bare feet slipping and sliding in the freezing mud.

Chapter Twenty-two

The day after Brian hit her, the area around Deanie's eye turned a dark purple, and makeup couldn't cover it up. Everyone—including her mother—bought into her story that she accidentally slipped in the snow and banged her face on the car bumper. Although things between her and Brian would never be the same, she still didn't want people thinking Brian had beaten her up.

A few days later, Deanie's mother confronted her about being pregnant. She had no doubt figured it out much earlier, but like Deanie, she probably stayed in denial as long as possible.

"Your breasts are swollen, Deanie," her mother said matter-of-factly as she came into the bathroom carrying towels.

Deanie was in the bathtub shampooing her hair, water dripping from the wet strands of hair onto her neck and shoulders. Surprised and embarrassed, Deanie quickly covered herself with her arms.

"I've noticed you've been filling out all over," her mother continued. "We shouldn't be blaming all your troubles on the flu, should we? You're in a motherly way, aren't you?"

Deanie looked away as her mother sat down on the edge of the tub.

For a moment, the small bathroom became awkwardly quiet, with only a slight dipping sound coming from the bathtub faucet. Deanie sat petrified, too embarrassed to look at her mother.

"I'm disappointed, Deanie," her mother said, making a disheartened sigh.

"Your father will be disappointed, too."

Finally, Deanie turned to her mother, her face white with fear. "Please don't tell Dad. He'll just go crazy."

"He'll find out sometime."

"Yes," Deanie cried. "But he'll think it was Brian's fault and go after him. It isn't Brian's fault; it's entirely mine."

"I hardly believe that, Deanie. Brian's as much to blame as you are."

In time, the drudgery of going to school became unbearable, yet Deanie forced herself out of bed each morning and got ready to go, checking in the mirror for changes in her body and wondering if anyone could tell. She avoided the Belles as much as she could. Her one class with Brian was the worst. She loved him and she knew he loved her, too, yet the anguish she saw in his eyes haunted her. She felt hopeless as what they should do.

Deanie's father got so enraged when he got the news, Deanie feared for Brian's life. On one of his rare days off, he vowed to go and find Brian and "kill the son-of-a-bitch." Deanie and her mother pleaded with him, but he got into his pickup with his shotgun. He was just backing up in the yard when Deanie, in desperation, ran up to his window and blurted out her promiscuity with both Brian and Bill Slater.

"I'm not sure who the father is!" she cried.

Her father's face changed from beat red to ash white. He looked off at his wife, standing beside the front door, looking downcast and bewildered. The agony of a broken heart seemed to resonate in both of them.

In the following days, Deanie's pregnancy began to show and her mother decided to visit the school principal to find out what options Deanie had in completing high school. Mr. Short was cordial and understanding. To spare Deanie embarrassment, he would arrange for Deanie's tests and assignments to be completed at home, using one of her friends as a courier. He said Deanie could still graduate if she dutifully completed her work. Mr. Short said he would also inform the school cheerleader director that Deanie would be withdrawing from the squad.

Deanie finally found the courage to call Karen. She worried that Karen might not want to be friends anymore. But when Karen answered the phone, Deanie was relieved to hear her say she was glad she called and that she missed her. Deanie also sensed that Karen was having troubles of her own. They agreed to go for a ride in Deanie's car.

It was now the first of March. Drifts of snow had accumulated to over a foot on the lawns and boulevards. The streets were still slick with snowpack and temperatures remained cold. Deanie disliked driving on slick roads, but cars were the one place she felt secure to talk in privacy. The wind was blowing hard and as the sun descended, the air became freezing cold. Deanie wished that another Chinook would come through.

Karen looked unhappy when she opened Deanie's Chevy door. She wore her black winter coat. Her blonde hair was pulled back into a ponytail with a scarf tied tightly over her head. Deanie could tell she had been crying.

"Gee, what's wrong, Karen? I thought only I had troubles."

"Oh, it's Dick," Karen said. "You won't believe what he's been doing."

Deanie drove up Park Street. She honked as they went by the Standard Station, although Brian was somewhere inside, out of sight, and probably getting ready to close up. She hoped he'd call her later.

"Dick told me he had a part-time job in the afternoons," Karen continued. "It's some part-time job, all right—part-time screwing the whores out at the whorehouse."

"What?" Deanie turned to Karen.

"Yeah, Linda found out from her brother, Greg, that he saw Dick leaving one of the rooms out there the other night. He asked around and found out that Dick's been practically living out there."

"Are you still seeing him?"

Karen shrugged. Her eyes were blurry and her voice trailed off. "I saw him today, but he doesn't say much to me anymore. I think he's punishing me."

Deanie made her way down Main Street. City plows had cleared much of the snowpack, and the drag seemed an ideal place to drive.

"It's kind of like, damned if you do and damned if you don't," Deanie said. "There's too much pressure not to screw these guys."

"I know," Karen said, rolling her eyes. "All the other Belles have gone all the way now. When you were home sick for a while, the other Belles all got together and talked. We really got together to talk about you, but Colleen, Rita, and Sherry admitted they weren't virgins any longer. Rita and Sherry did it on a double date last New Year's Eve, in the same car, at the same time. Now Colleen's back with her old boyfriend from Billings, and they're doing it now. I'm the last of the Mohicans. Our sexy little Linda has done it so often, she's off the charts."

"She's definitely going to win the contest, isn't she," Deanie grinned.

"We should have changed the contest from how many guys we felt to how many guys we screwed," Karen said, laughing.

"Why were you guys talking about me?" Deanie asked, sure she already knew.

"We've been concerned about how you have kind of dropped out of the club," Karen said nervously. "And there have been rumors floating around."

Deanie sighed. "I suppose there has. I wanted to tell you, Karen. It's just that I've been so ashamed."

Deanie stopped her car in front of the J. C. Penney building. She wiped her eyes with the sleeve of her jacket.

"I'm about four months along, Karen."

Karen moved across the seat and hugged her. "I'm so sorry, Deanie. Does Brian know?"

"Yes, he knows everything now," Deanie said, crying.

"Please forgive me for asking this, Deanie, but is it Brian's?"

Deanie dropped her head in her hands and sobbed. "Oh, Karen, I don't know for sure, but it just has to be Brian's. It just has to."

After dropping off Karen, Deanie drove back down Park Street with the wind blowing fiercely at her back. Sunlight was fading away, and the sky was a deep black-purple. A westbound passenger train had just pulled into the depot, and Deanie could see the many faces in the windows. She wished she could be on that train, going somewhere, leaving everything and everyone behind.

Chapter Twenty-three

Brian agonized over Deanie. It might have been rape, but Deanie should not have been there to begin with. He hated Bill Slater, vowing that he wasn't going to get away with what he did. Deanie was pregnant, but he wouldn't let himself believe that Slater might be the father. He still loved Deanie, and he decided that it was better to have her and to hurt than to not have her at all. He struggled to accept what had happened, knowing nothing could ever change it, but the anguish just wouldn't leave him alone. His anger got so great, he wanted to lash out at Deanie, to punish her, make her feel the pain he felt. Each night after work, he'd pick her up at her house. They would drive around town for a few minutes before heading up on the Point or Willow Creek, where they'd make love, hoping that the lovemaking would make everything whole and good again. He couldn't concentrate on schoolwork, and he worried they might not let him graduate in the spring. He had no idea what he might do if he did graduate, but he knew he didn't want to go to school another year. He and his mother only seemed to cross paths in the mornings when she'd get up and fix him breakfast before he dashed off to school. His mother was dating a truck driver she met at the truck stop, and she seemed preoccupied with him. She did lecture Brian about his school and the late nights he kept, but Brian hardly listened. All he cared or thought about was Deanie and the wish to one day meet up with Bill Slater.

He seldom saw Dick, except for a few classes at school. Dick practically lived at the whorehouse. He had developed a relationship with Marianne and confessed that he had become tormented with jealously, too, each time Charlotte made Marianne go off and service another customer. They removed Dick's cast in January, but the leg wasn't mending properly.

By late March, the longer daylight hours brought a slight warming. The good news was that spring was coming; the bad news was that graduation was also coming, along with Deanie's baby.

One cold Sunday morning, Brian received a frantic phone call from Orlen at the station. It was five o'clock, an hour before Brian was supposed to open up. It wasn't unusual for Orlen to come in early to do his paperwork.

"Brian, where did you hide the money tray last night?" Orlen asked.

Brian quickly snapped himself awake. "In the backroom," Brian answered, thinking that he might have hid the tray a little too good the night before, perhaps piling on too many inner tubes. "Where we always hide it."

"Well, we've got a problem," Orlen said, his voice troubled. "Think you can come in a little early?"

Brian dressed as fast as he could. His mother offered him toast, but he flew by her and out into the cold morning air. There was only a hint of daylight in the sky as Brian sped down a deserted Park Street. The street had a few icy spots but was mostly clear. He wondered why Orlen couldn't find the money tray.

When Brian got to the station, the inside lights were on. Orlen's bulk truck was parked along one side of the pumps, while a sheriff's patrol car sat idling on the other side. Puzzled, Brian hurried inside. Orlen and a deputy sheriff were standing out in the service bay, seemingly waiting for Brian. The back window in the bay was wide open, letting the cold air rush in. The deputy held a black Kodak and busied himself by snapping photos of the bay area.

"Looks like they took all the cash but left the checks," the deputy said, looking around the bay at paper strewn across the floor and up against the car hoist.

Orlen stood motionless, his face pale with worry. In one hand, he held a white till tape. The other hand was tucked in the pocket of his heavy dark blue coat.

"Do you know anything about this, Brian?"

Brian saw puddles of frozen water still dotting the floor from when he hosed down the bay area the night before. Lying next to the hoist was the empty black plastic cash tray.

Brian gasped. "What happened?"

"Someone busted through that window," the deputy said. He walked toward the office. "I'd better call Sheriff McCarthy."

Orlen looked at the till tape. "We should have had almost a hundred eighty bucks in that till."

Brian walked to the backroom and saw that the used tires and inner tubes had been tossed aside as if someone had been looking for something. "No one but you and I knew where that tray was, Orlen," he said.

"The sheriff's coming right over," the deputy said. He stuck his head out the open window. "I see pry marks on the outside of this windowsill," he said, snapping pictures.

Sheriff McCarthy never got there until after seven. Brian had tried getting the station opened by hauling out the washbasin and oil racks, but the deputy stopped him, warning Brian not to tamper with evidence.

Sheriff McCarthy was wearing his white Stetson and a heavy gray parka over his tan shirt and trousers. His pistol bulged awkwardly under his parka. He didn't come inside right away. After parking his patrol car next to the office, he stopped to have a look at Brian's Chevy. From the office window, Brian watched him write in a notebook. When he came inside, he said good morning to Orlen but remained mostly quiet as he strolled about the premises. He instructed the deputy to look around outside and then stepped up to Brian. He asked Brian to give him his name and he wrote that in his notebook.

The sheriff motioned for Brian to sit in the chair next to the office desk while he stood by the stove, rubbing his hands together, making Brian very nervous.

"What do you know about the missing money, West?" His voice was much too accusatory.

"Now wait a minute, Sheriff McCarthy," Brian said, rising from the chair. "All I know is that I hid the money where we always do."

The sheriff became angry. "Sit down in that chair!" he shouted, his face turning red. "If you don't cooperate, we'll do this at my jailhouse."

Brian sat down angrily. Orlen had gone outside to move his bulk truck and to assist customers who were lining up for gas.

Sheriff McCarthy walked across the room and peered out the side window of the office. "Is that your Chevy parked out there, West?"

Brian nodded.

"You know, I deal with young guys like you all the time," the sheriff said. "It amazes me how some of you turn out pretty good and some of you go bad. There seems to be a crossroad you guys hit about your age. Why some of you take the wrong road, I don't know." Finally, he turned from the window to face Brian. "Maybe you know something about this robbery or maybe you don't, West, but I've been looking for a thief in this county."

Brian's heart was beating so fast, he thought he had just run a hundred yard dash. He coughed nervously.

"This thief has been stealing beer off distribution trucks. One sixteen-gallon keg turned up over at the Bozeman school grounds the night their football field caught on fire. The truck driver claims he delivered all the kegs on his truck, but the Mint Bar owner insists he's missing two sixteen-gallon kegs. It would seem that a thief intercepted them."

Brian shook his head nervously. "Believe me, Sheriff, it wasn't me."

"It just happens a car matching the description of your Chevy out there, right down to that big dent in the trunk lid, was spotted over there that night. One of those missing kegs fell out of someone's vehicle. Perhaps it was your vehicle, West."

Brian slouched in the chair. He suddenly felt sick to his stomach.

"And now we have this robbery," the sheriff said. "Could the same thief be involved?"

The deputy sheriff came back into the office after investigating from outside. "I found some fresh shoeprints in the snow under the open window," he said, his eyes trained on Brian's loafers. "Whoever was out there wore metal cleats on the heels of his shoes."

Brian felt faint.

"Let's see the bottoms of those shoes you're wearing, West," the sheriff demanded.

Brian quickly slipped off his shoes and handed them to him.

"Well," Sheriff McCarthy said, smiling. "Wouldn't you know it, there are cleats on the bottoms of your heels."

Chapter Twenty-four

They didn't put Brian in a jail cell, although he worried they would as he rode in the back seat of Sheriff McCarthy's patrol car. They had taken both of his shoes, and he had to walk barefoot into the sheriff's office. Instead of a cell, he spent most of the day in a hardwood chair in front of the sheriff's desk.

"You're damn lucky you're only seventeen, West," the sheriff said. "One year older and you'd be back there in the tank."

Brian's denial of any wrongdoing was going on deaf ears, and the sheriff and deputies all took turns trying to get him to confess, not only for the station robbery but also the beer heist.

The sheriff finally called Brian's mom at the truck stop around noontime. She rushed right over, her face flushed with alarm.

"Brian wouldn't do anything like that," she said. "Would he?"

She stayed in the office for over an hour and then left back for work after the sheriff told her she couldn't take him home yet.

When his mother left, it occurred to Brian that even she wasn't convinced he was innocent. He began to feel hopelessly alone. The deputy let him use the telephone, and he tried to call Dick. He wasn't surprised that his mother said he wasn't home. Frustrated, his next call was to Deanie. It was awkward telling her he had been arrested. He worried that she too might not believe him. She was surprised at what he told her, but she said she wholeheartedly stood behind him. She asked if he wanted her to come to the sheriff's office. He told her no. She said she would try and find Dick.

It wasn't until after five that the sheriff came into his office, carrying Brian's loafers. He tossed them at Brian's feet and sat down at his desk.

"I'm clearing you of the station robbery for now, West," he said, not a bit apologetic. "The shoeprints are larger than yours."

Brian sighed in relief. He quickly pulled on his loafers. Smiling, he reached out to shake the sheriff's hand.

75

The sheriff took Brian's hand unemotionally. "You're still on the list for the beer, though. Why don't we discuss how your car and a keg of stolen beer happened to be on that football field at the same time?"

Disappointed, Brian slumped back down in the chair. His mind raced. Instinctively, he knew he shouldn't tell what he knew about the beer. He pictured the big, angry face of Dan Buckley.

"Are you afraid of any reprisals, West?" the sheriff asked.

Brian shook his head. "I don't know who the thief is, Sheriff McCarthy."

"Just so you know, West, I never give up on a case. Sooner or later, I get my man."

At seven P.M., the county juvenile officer came into the office. He was a little more understanding than the sheriff, but he still wanted to know about the beer. He questioned Brian for another hour until they decided to let him go.

No one offered to give him a ride back to the station, but Brian hardly cared. All he wanted was to get out of there. He could have called Deanie, but he didn't want to take the time. When they said he could go, he rushed out into the cold night air. It was disheartening that those close to him—especially his mother and Orlen—would think he'd do anything like that. He was cleared of the robbery, but he wondered if he still had a job. He didn't know what he was going to do about the beer. Buckley probably stole it, but he didn't want to be a squealer.

The station was only a few blocks away and Brian walked fast, hunching up his shoulders and keeping his hands tucked in the pockets of his letterman's jacket. Dick was probably at the whorehouse, bedded down with Marianne and oblivious to any trouble. Across Park Street, he heard the clang from the switch engine bell. There were only a few cars on the street, but a semi roared by, crunching the clumps of ice that still lingered.

Then, out of nowhere, a silver Oldsmobile pulled in from behind him, stopping abruptly at the curb. He didn't recognize the car at first but then realized it was Dick driving his mother's car.

Dick's voice rang out from the window, "Need a lift?"

"Man, you could have gotten here a little sooner," Brian said, eagerly sliding inside the warm car.

"Sorry, buddy," Dick said, pulling away from the curb. "Actually, I just got the word. I hurried down to the sheriff's office to either bail you out or bust you out."

"I didn't think anything could get you away from Marianne."

"Hey, man, there's more to life than pussy."

Brian laughed. "Since when?"

"So why were you in jail?"

"They thought I robbed the station," Brian said. He raised his foot and pointed to his loafer. "Whoever broke in wore steel cleats on his heels. He also had a pretty good idea where the money was hidden." Suddenly, it dawned on him that Dick wore cleats on his shoes, too.

Oddly, Dick was silent for a time. Finally, he said, "Hell, half the kids at school wear cleat on their heels." Dick turned into the station and parked alongside Brian's Chevy.

Brian pulled on the door latch and said, "I know they do, Dick. And that includes you."

"What is that supposed to mean?" Dick asked.

"I don't know what that means, Dick," Brian said, stepping out of the Buick. "I don't even want to think about what that could mean."

He found the keys under the front seat and started the car, letting the motor warm up. Surprisingly, Dick hadn't backed away and he soon appeared next to Brian's window.

"I'm sorry, Brian. I let you down."

Brian looked out at him. "You did this? Did you?"

"I needed the money, Brian. Charlotte said I had to pay my tab out there or she'd call the sheriff."

"You son-of-a-bitch!" Brian blurted out.

He pushed open the car door, shoving Dick back against the Oldsmobile. Brian landed a blow to Dick's jaw and pushed him across the car hood. He hit him once more, but Dick wouldn't fight back.

Dick's nose was bleeding. "Hit me all you want. I deserve it."

"What kind of friend would do something like this?"

"You've got to believe me, Brian. I didn't think they'd suspect you."

"Well, they did, you stupid bastard. What the hell am I going to do now?"

Dick looked up, his face smeared with blood. "Nothing, Brian. Don't do anything. They can't get you for this. They won't get me either if you keep quiet."

"I work here," Brian said, pointing to the station. "Orlen gave me a job. He was good to me."

"Orlen will be okay," Dick said. "He'll get insurance money. In time, this will all blow over."

Brian felt a pounding in his head. "Did you know that the beer Buckley had the night of the kegger was stolen?"

Dick shook his head. "That doesn't surprise me."

"Well, the sheriff thinks I stole it. The Bozeman cops identified my car. Either I tell them who brought the beer or I get busted with illegal possession."

"It'll be okay, Brian. You haven't done anything wrong."

Brian got back inside his car. Dick called out to him, but he didn't hear or care what he said. The night sky was clear. A rising moon was a soft glow behind the mountains to the southeast. Brian hadn't eaten all day and his stomach hurt. He started out going down to Deanie's house but then decided to go on home.

Chapter Twenty-five

That Monday, Deanie began her home study program. The morning sky was bright and clear. From her living room window, she watched for Karen to stop by and pick up her English assignment. She was glad she didn't have to face all the inquisitive eyes at school while she was dressed in her snug-fitting clothes over her protruding tummy. By now, she was totally devoted to Brian, but the awful ache she carried in her side just wouldn't go away. Being in love wasn't entirely a wonderful thing. Along with the warmth of lovemaking, she endured the jealous rages of Brian. Inevitably, after they had extinguished their nightly passion for each other, Brian would obsess over Bill Slater and question her over and over about details she neither could nor wanted to remember. He would sometimes shout at her and call her names, until she would finally break into hysterical sobs and at last he would become quiet, enduring the pain by himself. She came to understand those moments. She knew he was hurt and blinded by a rage neither of them could do anything about.

When they held him under suspicion of robbery, she waited nervously for him to call. She knew he wouldn't have done that to Orlen and they would have to release him. But when the day got late and he hadn't called, she went looking for him. Surprisingly, she found his car parked in front of his house. She let herself in the back door and found him in a sour mood. He'd been crying. She snuggled up to him, wrapping her arms around him. He didn't want to talk about the station being robbed, saying only that he didn't have anything to do with it. She believed him, although she wondered what difference it would have made if he had actually robbed the station.

After a while, Brian lay down on the couch and as he rested, she busied herself washing some dishes that lay in the kitchen sink and straightening up the house a little. She thought about Brian's mother and the difficulty she must have to endure to raise a son without a husband, working long hours

79

just to get by. It occurred to her that she might meet the same fate. Soon she realized she was as depressed as Brian. He was snoring softly when she finally left for home.

Now, sitting in her living room, waiting for Karen, she started to worry about Brian, aching for him as well as for her. When Karen drove into the driveway in her mother's car, Deanie rushed out to greet her. Karen looked fresh and pretty, dressed in a pleated brown skirt with a matching bow in her hair. The air inside the car was warm and filled with the sweet scent of Karen's perfume. Deanie stretched across the seat to hug her.

"I'm so glad to see you," Deanie said, placing her English assignment on the seat between them.

"So how's the pregnant lady?" Karen asked, smiling, her bright teeth gleaming.

"Oh, don't ask," Deanie said, scowling. "Life's a bitch. I feel like a fat old cow."

Karen laughed. "Well, you still look beautiful to me."

"Did you hear about the station?" Deanie asked.

Karen nodded. She looked away through the windshield. "I know all about it now. I was with Dick last night. He told me everything."

"Really, Dick came over?"

"Yes. He had his mom's car and we drove up on the Point for a while. He was really depressed. We were only going to talk, but other things happened, too."

Deanie turned sharply to Karen. "What other things?"

Karen's face reddened. She nervously nibbled on her bottom lip. "I finally gave into him, Deanie."

Deanie sat quietly, staring out at the snow still thick on the lawn. She sighed and looked at Karen. "Are you okay with it?"

Karen shrugged. Her eyes watered. "I guess so. I can't do anything about it now. I love him—I always have."

"I know you do," Deanie said. "Don't feel badly about it. It was bound to happen sooner or later."

"Dick sure knew what he was doing," Karen chuckled. She pulled a tissue from her purse and carefully dabbed at her eyes. "I guess spending all that time with whores taught him a lot. I was vulnerable, anyway." Karen pulled up her coat sleeve to check her wristwatch. "Dick and Brian had quite a talk last night. That's why Dick was feeling so down."

"Why was he so down?"

"Because of what he did," Karen said, looking surprised that Deanie had asked. "You mean Brian didn't tell you?"

Deanie shook her head.

"Well, you have a right to know," Karen said. "Dick was the one who robbed the station."

"No way!" Deanie blurted.

Karen looked at her watch again. "I have to go."

Deanie pushed open the door. "I just can't believe it, Karen. Please call me later."

Chapter Twenty-six

Despite his mother's nagging, Brian stayed in his house for two days, lying on his bed, thinking about things or sleeping, at least until the sun went down. He had no interest in school or work. It was odd feeling angry at so many people at the same time. He dwelled on the fact that those most important to him had betrayed him at least once, including Deanie, Orlen, his mother, and now Dick. But it was Deanie who hurt him the most, and he wondered if his feelings for Deanie were more hatred than love. And he worried about what he was going to do after graduation. He'd think about marrying Deanie, working on the railroad, like his grandfather did, making a life for them. Then he'd think about Deanie being pregnant, perhaps by another man. The anguish was so overwhelming some days that the only way he found he could cope with it was to fantasize about beating Bill Slater senseless.

The telephone rang several times over the next two days. The school called to find out where he was and to tell him Mr. Short wanted to talk with him as soon as possible. Dick called again and again, but Brian kept hanging up on him. Orlen never did call.

Each night after sundown, Brian would drive down to Deanie's house, always finding her eagerly waiting for him. Seeing her bundled in her winter coat and scarf, he wondered if spring would ever come. It seemed it had always been winter. That Tuesday night, he drove up to the Point, parking near the remains of an old forgotten campfire. Most of the snow had either blown away or melted off, and surprisingly, the ground was fairly dry. The wind was still fierce and cold, and Brian kept the heater on high. The Salt Lake radio station was coming in clear, and for a time they listened to Elvis singing *"It's Now or Never"* as they looked out over the lights of town below. A Northern Pacific engine was pulling out of the rail yard, towing a long line of freight cars, snaking eastward across the railroad bridge.

"Karen told me about Dick," Deanie said. "About him robbing the station."

"Dick should keep his mouth shut," Brian said.

"What are you going to do about it?"

Brian shrugged. "I don't want to talk about Dick."

"Okay, we won't talk."

She turned and kissed him on the cheek and then began removing her blouse. When she was undressed, she snuggled up against him. Her body was changing, and Brian wondered at what point they should stop making love. He wrapped his arms around her, enjoying her warmth. He removed his clothes and nudged her down in the seat. The heater was blowing out warm air, and the radio continued to come in clearly.

It wasn't long before Brian heard the low whine of a vehicle laboring to make the grade to the Point. He lay still, alertly listening as the vehicle made the crest, grinding its gears. It wasn't until Brian heard the vehicle pull up next to him that Brian reached for his shirt and sat upright in the car seat. Deanie stayed down on the seat. Suddenly, there was a rap on the window. Deanie screeched and grabbed for her clothes, spreading them across her body.

It was Dick.

"What the hell do you want?" Brian snapped as he rolled down the window.

"Sorry," Dick said. "I need to talk to you."

"Well, I'm a little busy right now."

Dick smiled. "I see that. I've been trying to call you. I had a hunch you'd be up here."

"I don't have much to say to you, Dick," Brian said, struggling to get his pants on.

Dick squatted in front of window, the wind ruffling his hair. "Will you step out here a sec?"

Brian noticed that Dick was driving his dad's pickup. Karen was sitting in the front seat. When he was dressed, he opened the door and stepped out into the cold wind but quickly reached back for his letterman's jacket. He walked to the rear of the Chevy, where Dick waited.

"I really don't want to talk with you, Dick. I'm still pissed."

"I know. I don't blame you. I screwed up—big time. I realize now I've been thinking with the wrong head."

"So, what is it?"

"So, I want to make it up to you," Dick said, bowing his head. "I'll turn myself in, if you want."

"You'll end up in jail."

"I know," Dick said. "I just feel so damn bad about what I did."

Brian remained silent.

"I found out something you might like to know, Brian."

"What's that?"

"You know this Bill Slater dude you've been itching to a get a piece of?"

"Yeah."

"Well, remember the night we saw his car out at the cathouse?"

Brian nodded.

"I had a chance to talk to Charlotte about him. She told me Slater works for some sort of escort service in California that operates a network of girls, extending all the way up here in Montana."

"You mean Slater's a pimp?"

"I guess so. Every few months he brings a couple of new girls up here from California and takes a few back with him. Charlotte says his job is to recruit new girls, especially from the high schools."

Brian glanced through the rear window. Deanie had her clothes on and was sitting up in the seat, chatting with Karen, sitting in the pickup.

"You back with Karen again?" he asked.

Dick grinned. "Yes. She finally let me screw her."

"Well, lucky you," Brian said sarcastically.

"Remember Marianne?" Dick asked. "She's scheduled to go back to California with Slater on his next visit up here."

"Too bad for you."

"I'm sure you realize this Slater is pretty interested in the Belles."

"I know," Brian said. "Especially Deanie."

"Now I want this guy as much as you do, Brian," Dick said. "Marianne told me Slater actually beat her up when she first refused to come up here to Livingston. I think this guy's a real badass."

"All the more reason to beat the shit out of him," Brian said.

"Charlotte says he's been coming to Livingston every spring and fall."

Brian rested his foot on the back bumper. He looked off toward the west and the lights of town. The cold night air hung like a haze over the lights, making the town seem even smaller. "I hate that guy," he said. "I wish he'd come back sooner."

Chapter Twenty-seven

The next day, Brian decided to face the music and go back to school. He was awake most of the night, formulating a plan to get Bill Slater back in town. By morning he had one, and during his morning classes he drafted a letter for Deanie to mail off to Slater. The letter had to offer sexual rewards, yet be convincing that it was actually Deanie's thoughts. By lunch, he had a draft ready for Deanie to rewrite, certain it would lure Slater back. He couldn't wait to rush down to her house over the lunch hour and give it to her. It never occurred to him that she might object.

"I can't send a letter like this, Brian," Deanie said, after reading the draft. "I don't have feelings like that."

"It doesn't matter," Brian shrugged. "The end justifies the means. I want him back here so I can beat him half to death."

"What then, Brian?" Deanie said, her voice rising. "Whether you beat him up or not, you're still going to be tormented with hate and jealously. It won't change anything."

"Damn it, Deanie. Just write it."

Brian's first class after lunch was World History. The teacher was Mr. Wolfe, Brian's least favorite teacher, who was eager to hand Brian a notice from the principal when Brian entered the classroom. Brian was to report to the principal's office immediately.

The principal's office was on the second floor and when Brian arrived, the door to Mr. Short's office was closed. The secretary had him sit in one of the office chairs to wait. After a few minutes, the door opened and Mr. Short waved him in.

Mr. Short shuffled through some papers on his desk until he found what he was looking for. "This is a transcript of your grades, Brian. And they don't look very good."

"I know," Brian said. "I'm trying to get them up."

"You're running out of time, Brian. Graduation is only two months from now. I'd hate to have to hold you over another year."

There was a burning sensation in Brian's stomach. He couldn't imagine another year of school.

"I also know about your troubles with Deanie Cummings," Mr. Short went on. "Your troubles seem to be multiplying. You had better be getting your life together, Brian."

When Brian left the office to go back to the World History class, he was more depressed than ever. Had Dan Buckley not been seated one row over and two desks back, he'd have laid his head on his desk and cried.

Mr. Short's talk convinced Brian that it was time to get back to studying. As soon as his last class let out, he hurried over to his locker and loaded his arms with every text and notebook he had. He couldn't imagine flunking his senior year.

Dick met him at the front doors and carried a few of his books. Cold air blasted them when they stepped outside.

"Are we having finals or something?" Dick asked.

"I'm flunking everything."

They loaded the books in the back seat of Brian's car. Brian was a little perturbed when Dick nonchalantly seated himself in the front seat.

"Give me a ride home?" Dick asked.

"I suppose," Brian said hesitantly. "I'll drop you off. I'm sure you don't want to go to the station with me. Hell, I'm not sure I want to go there, either."

"I suppose not," Dick said.

His face grew pale. Brian knew he had hurt his feelings.

Neither of them spoke until Brian turned east on Park Street. The street was clear of snow, but mounds of it lay along the curb.

"I'm trying, Brian," Dick said. "We've been friends a long time. I'll make it up to you somehow."

"Don't you realize that because I know you robbed the station, by not telling I'm as guilty as you are?"

"I know," Dick said. "Please give me another chance."

Brian didn't answer; his thoughts turned to what he was going to say to Orlen.

When they pulled up to Dick's house, Dick turned to Brian and said, "I've got an idea about Bill Slater."

"Don't be concerned about him," Brian said quickly. "I'll take care of the asshole myself."

"I know you can, but you can't kill him. I've been thinking of a way to get him thrown in jail."

"How's that going to happen?"

"Not sure yet, but it involves that shiny red car of his and Dan Buckley."

"I hate that car," Brian said. "Whenever I visualize him humping Deanie in it, I want to take a sledge to it."

Dick opened the car door to leave. "I need to talk to Buckley. I'll talk to you more about it later."

One block from the station, Brian almost turned around. He couldn't imagine what he was going to say to Orlen. When he got there, Orlen was bent over, checking a customer's tire pressure, while a new Mercury sat idling on the other side of the pumps. The office was crowded with customers. Brian snapped up his jacket and walked over to Orlen, unsure how things would turn out.

"Am I glad to see you," Orlen said, glancing up at Brian.

Brian was instantly uplifted. "What needs to be done with the Mercury?" he asked.

"Fill it with high-test," Orlen said. "And check under the hood. I'll work on this one."

"Yes, sir," Brian said enthusiastically.

Business was brisk until six-thirty, when Orlen finally decided to close up. The only change in the operations was that the cash was no longer being kept at the station overnight. When Brian left that night, it was the best he felt all week.

Brian's mother was away when Brian got home. He made himself a bologna sandwich. He talked to Deanie on the phone, telling her about his meeting with Mr. Short. He told her he was going to study. When he asked her about the letter to Bill Slater, she told him she had written the letter and mailed it off. He was pleased with her, never questioning her about what she had written. They each said I love you before hanging up.

Chapter Twenty-eight

By her fifth month, Deanie was totally disgusted in the way she looked. She hadn't gained much in her legs and thighs, but her breasts were bulging and her tummy protruded out sharply, *looking more like a beach ball every day,* she thought. She felt sick most of the time and sometimes—especially at night—she'd get dreadfully depressed. She was becoming more and more convinced the baby was Bill's. She worried that Brian sensed it, too, wondering why he stayed with her. Did he truly love her, or was he sticking around merely to one day garner some sort of revenge against Bill? She loved him and hoped that love would carry them through.

When Brian gave her a draft of a letter he wanted her to write, she waited until she was safely inside her bedroom before tearing it into a hundred pieces. She never wanted to hear from or see Bill Slater again. If he should return, there was a chance he'd tell Brian about their romantic episodes. Brian could hardly handle the little mischief he already knew about; any more of it would destroy him completely and any chance of their future together. She thought about how badly she had messed up her life. She was thankful for her supporting family and friends, but she wished she didn't have to depend so heavily on them. She managed to keep her grades up, and she enjoyed talking with Karen whenever she'd stop by. The highlight of each day was when she could be with Brian. She prayed that she'd hold on to him and that someday his rage would subside.

When school let out that afternoon, Deanie was delighted to see Colleen's blue Ford drive into the driveway with all the Belles inside. They were all cheerful, beaming with excitement about an idea they had. Deanie ushered them all into her small bedroom. Dressed in skirts and blouses, Deanie envied their slender figures.

"Everyone's been hinting about it," Karen said, smiling. "And now we're just going to do it."

"Do what?" Deanie asked.

"You are going to have a baby shower!" Rita blurted out.

Sherry was chomping vigorously on her gum. "It'll be so much fun."

"And we can even expand it into a slumber party, like the old days," Linda said.

Deanie was glad they were her friends. Sometimes they acted alike, dressed alike, but when she looked closely, each one of them were their own person. She wondered why she was the only one pregnant.

Deanie noticed Linda lying on the bed grinning, obviously tickled about something.

"I've got a big surprise for you guys," she said, giggling. "I can't keep it a secret much longer."

"Oh, Linda," Sherry quipped. "Why do you have all this intrigue about you?"

"I love shocking you guys," Linda said, smiling. "I'll show you at the slumber party."

Before the Belles all left, Karen handed Deanie her latest homework. "Now don't forget. The shower is this Saturday at seven at my house."

When they were gone, Deanie sat down on her bed. She began thinking about her pregnancy but less about herself and more about what pregnancy was really about: a baby, a delicate human baby growing inside her, with genes half hers and half the father's. No matter how desperate she willed Brian to be the father, it was still a baby, regardless.

They held the shower on March 25, as planned. La Belle Six and all their mothers were there. The A and B squad cheerleaders came, as did Sherry's two younger sisters, Colleen's older sister, and Karen's next-door neighbor. The dining room table held a variety of sandwiches, salads, cakes, candy, and cookies that the Belles prepared. Everyone made a guess as to when Deanie would have the baby, the winner to receive a ten-dollar gift certificate from J. C. Penney. Listening to the chatter about diapers, formula, and nursing, Deanie marveled at the differences in knowledge between the adults and teens. The topics discussed regarding having and caring for babies, and how they were expressed seemed worlds apart. It occurred to Deanie that those two worlds needed to be traversed rather quickly.

Thankfully, nobody brought up the subject of the baby's father. Deanie hoped everyone had just assumed that Brian was the father, but when no one brought up Brian's name, she got a little worried that perhaps they too weren't sure. Colleen's mother did mention Brian. As she was leaving, she told Deanie to give her best to him. The shower ended around nine. Those leaving all gave Deanie a hug and wished her luck.

Deanie's mother was the last to leave, telling Deanie not to stay up too late at the slumber party. "You need your rest," she told Deanie.

The other Belles remained in good spirits, each of them helping Karen's mother pick up the house. Normally at their slumber parties, they'd popped popcorn, but they all agreed that they were still too full from all the goodies they ate at the party. By ten, La Belle Six secluded themselves in Karen's bedroom, quickly changing into their pajamas. Deanie slipped into her loosefitting, red cotton trousers with a matching jacket, while the others donned their regular revealing baby-doll nighties. Each of them flipped through Karen's pile of 45 rpm records, searching for their favorite songs to play on Karen's phonograph.

Deanie was enjoying herself, but she couldn't help think about Brian. She was used to seeing him almost every night. Making love was her reassurance. But her friends were important, too. She loved them and enjoyed their company even though she was beginning to feel like an old married lady around them. The Belles could behave like grownups when they had to, but they still enjoyed acting up, being silly, and giggling about guys.

It wasn't long before Karen locked her bedroom door and reached under her bed to retrieve two large bottles of grape wine, along with a stack of paper cups. Linda squealed when she saw the wine. Sherry passed out the Lucky Strike cigarettes, and soon the small room was filled with smoke. With their drinks in hand, they jitterbugged and twisted around the room to Elvis, Fats Domino, and Jerry E. Lewis. The smoke became increasingly dense, and Karen opened both of her bedroom windows. Not only did the smoke flow out, but so did the music. Karen's mom had to pound on the door for them to turn the music down. This was the time that Linda decided to spring her big surprise on her friends. Karen turned down the phonograph, and everyone eagerly plopped down on the bed.

"You're all going to just die," Linda said, bubbling over with excitement, her blue eyes sparkling. From her overnight bag, she removed a large yellow envelope and laid it in the middle of the bed. "Check this out."

The girls formed a circle around the envelope, which was addressed to Linda. Deanie was quick to notice the California return address. Slowly, Linda slid out two eight-by-ten, black-and-white photographs, one on top of the other, creating a chorus of gasps from everyone.

The top photo showed a beautiful young woman, clad in an elegant black low-cut gown, poised in what appeared to be the backseat of a limousine. Her long dark hair was piled in a professional coiffure. Strings of white pearls dangled from her earlobes and draped across her bosom and wrists. In one hand she gracefully held a long-stemmed wine glass, filled with clear bubbly liquid. In her other hand she gripped the erect penis of a man, his face unseen off camera.

Deanie felt a burn on her own face as she watched her friend's faces turn red. She couldn't believe what she was seeing.

"Where in the world did you get this?" Colleen said, completely surprised.

Linda laughed. "You haven't seen anything yet." Smirking, she transferred the bottom picture to the top.

In this picture, it was the same girl in the same setting, grasping the penis, but now her face was positioned much closer to it. The camera captured her wet tongue curled, just inches away from the penis, posed as if the girl had just taken a lick from a strawberry ice cream cone.

"These can't be real," Sandy said, shaking her head.

"Of course, they're real," Linda snapped. "How else did they get the pictures?"

"Real or not," Colleen said, grinning, "they do what they were intended to do."

"Yeah," Rita said. "Like, get you all hot and bothered."

Deanie felt lightheaded. She couldn't get the California address off her mind. It must have come from Bill Slater.

"My God, Linda," Karen said. "Where did you get these?"

Linda was clearly enjoying herself. She reached back inside the envelope and pulled out a letter. "Listen to this," she said as she started to read:

Dear Linda

The girl's name is Dani. She works for the same company I do. She graduated from high school two years ago. Last year she earned over twenty-five thousand dollars, and she's having the time of her life. I've asked Deanie to try and get La Belle Six to come out here and work with us. It's a glamorous business. Dani has done modeling and has even been in TV commercials. Believe it or not, Hollywood is interested in her. This is the kind of business you can pretty much do what you are comfortable with. Besides modeling, you can accompany men to various functions and parties. There is no obligation to do anything you don't want to, but if there is anything that interests you (like Dani here), you can do that, too.

La Belles will be graduating soon, and this would be a great career for all of you. My company only hires attractive girls like the Belles. I hope you can convince Deanie and the rest to consider the job. It sure beats trying to eke out a living in Livingston. Here, you might even meet that Mr. Right.

Let me hear from you.

Your friend,

Bill.

Deanie's lightheadedness soon turned into dizziness as she sat listening to Linda read the letter. Her heart pounded and sweat beads trickled down between her breasts. There was a churning sensation in her stomach, and the room suddenly began to reel. She dashed for one of the open windows, throwing her head out over the sill. Abruptly, bites of cake, cookies, and candies— all colored in purple wine—splashed down the outside of Karen's house.

Chapter Twenty-nine

Brian discovered that if he just read the words in his US history text, without frustrating himself in trying to memorize the names, dates, and places, history was actually interesting. It interrupted his learning trend when he had to stop and read the details several times in hopes he'd remember them. History was his worst class, primarily because he hated the teacher, Mr. Wolfe. It was obvious that Mr. Wolfe didn't like him, either.

"If you don't start paying attention in this class, West," he informed Brian one day, "I'm going to flunk you, and I'll enjoy doing it."

Despite Mr. Wolfe, Brian was determined to pass the course. With a test scheduled the next Friday, Brian immersed himself in the Civil War. By test time, he felt more confident about the prospects of passing a test than at any other time. His studying had paid off, and he sailed through the true-and-false and multiple-choice questions with ease. Amazingly, he even had something to write about on the essay question regarding Sherman's march to the sea. When Brian walked out of class, he was satisfied that he did well enough to at least get a passing grade.

The next day at school, a contingent of military recruiters had set up tables near the principal's office. With the U.S. flag and the representative flags of the Army, Navy, Air Force, and Marines positioned behind them, four impeccably dressed military officers sat in folding chairs, handing out pamphlets. Brian had just stepped out of his English class and noticed several guys grouped around the tables, looking at the pamphlets and listening to the recruiters. When he spotted Dick there, Brian hurried over beside him.

"So, what do you think?" Brian asked.

Dick handed Brian one of the pamphlets. "This Army one talks about a buddy plan. Says if you and a buddy enlist together, you stay together."

Brian quickly scanned the colored pamphlet. "Kind of makes enlistment look a little easier, doesn't it?"

"Yeah," Dick said enthusiastically. "They don't say where in the world you'll end up, but I guess if you're with a friend, it really doesn't matter."

Brian folded the pamphlet and shoved it into his back pocket. He rushed off to his next class. Just as he turned to enter the classroom, big Dan Buckley met him at the doorway, smiling, his gold front teeth gleaming.

"Hello, West," Buckley said. His voice had an odd, pleasant tone to it. "I was talking to Dana about this dude from California who drives the fancy red Bonneville."

Dick said he was going to talk with Buckley, but it surprised Brian that he did it so soon. He wasn't entirely comfortable with an alliance with Buckley and wondered how much Dick had divulged.

"Yeah, his name is Bill Slater. All I want to do is beat the piss out of him."

"I'm sure you're capable, West," Buckley said. "But I'd like to be your backup should you need it."

"Don't bother yourself, Buckley. I can fight my own battles."

"Hey, I didn't mean to make you mad. I'm trying to be friendly. Anyway, Dana has a plan that might help you, him, and me at the same time."

The period bell was about to ring, and Brian stepped around Buckley to enter the room. He shrugged, telling Buckley, "I just want a piece of Slater. What you and Dick do is up to you."

Chapter Thirty

By the end of April, Brian's grades were improving, as was the weather. The ground snow had all melted off, and precipitation was no longer snow but a mixture of sleet and rain. Winter was losing ground and spring was in sight. The trees were budding, and the open fields showed signs of new grass with young gophers scampering about them. Although the wind continued to howl, the air was feeling much warmer.

Brian missed seeing Deanie at school. Once he started studying, they had to forego much of their nightly lovemaking. One Friday, in mid-May, the seniors were supposed to have a dress-up day, where the guys wore suits and ties and the girls wore fancy dresses with frilly hats. Since he didn't own a suit, Brian decided to skip school and to take Deanie for a ride in the country. Before he left his house, he grabbed his .22 rifle in case he saw any gophers. Since he hadn't fired the rifle in over a year, he thought it might be fun to get in some target practice. The lever-action rifle was given to him by his grandfather. Gopher hunting was one of the fun activities they done together.

"You have to get them in the springtime," his grandfather had told him. "When the grass gets tall, you won't be able to see them."

In the afternoon, Brian drove Deanie and him south along the Yellowstone River and into Paradise Valley. The sky was blue and clear of clouds, and the sun's warmth had cancelled out the coolness of the wind. Deanie was dressed in slacks and wore her hooded jacket. Brian marveled over how filled out she was. It seemed like the baby could come at any time.

The fields all swarmed with gophers, and Brian waited until he found a dry spot to pull off the highway. He found a good place a few miles from Chico Hot Springs, where hundreds of gophers scampered about a large open pasture field and parked alongside a rusty barbwire fence.

As he stepped out of the car with his rifle, it occurred to him that Deanie had never been on a gopher hunt and probably had no idea what he was doing. He rested the rifle on one of the posts and motioned for Deanie to come out to watch. Brian injected a shell into the rifle and was taking aim on a gopher resting on his rump some thirty yards into the field.

He was about to squeeze off a shot when Deanie said, very innocently, "You're not going to shoot one of those cute little things, are you?"

Her childlike question almost floored him. He had never heard anyone say that before, and it never occurred to him that it was wrong to kill gophers. His grandfather and any farmer or rancher he ever talked to considered gophers pests, akin to mice and rats, ruining the fields for crops and livestock. All Brian could say was, "Huh?"

"They remind me of this guinea pig I had once," Deanie said calmly. "Why would you shoot them?"

With that sentence, Deanie ended Brian's gopher-hunting days forever. If he was to ever take aim on another gopher again, he'd remember her asking that one question: "Why?"

After a change of heart, Brian gathered up some beer and pop cans scattered near the road and walked out in the field several yards to line them up. Since he came out to target practice, the cans were the next best thing. Deanie seemed to enjoy watching Brian hit the cans, making them pop up in the air. Soon she decided she wanted to try it herself and was eager for Brian to show her how to operate the rifle. They spent the rest of the afternoon there, using up three boxes of shells. As the sun faded, Brian considered looking for a secluded place to park, to perhaps make love, but then he thought about the shape Deanie was in and decided that lovemaking was no longer wise. They drove back to town, making small talk and listening to the radio. Brian never once mentioned Bill Slater.

Chapter Thirty-one

Two days before graduation, Karen called Deanie in mid-afternoon to tell her that Bill Slater was back in town. Linda's brother spotted Bill's red Pontiac out at the whorehouse. Deanie was ill at the time. She was well into her seventh month by then. Oddly, she felt hungry most of the time, but often after she ate, she vomited it up. Weary of being pregnant and confined mostly to her bedroom, she became acutely depressed. She longed to finally give birth to her baby, wondering if it was a boy or a girl, worrying who it might look like.

The news had a paralyzing effect on Deanie. She knew he'd return sometime, but then, at that moment, she just wasn't ready. She gasped for breath and for a moment, she couldn't speak. Karen kept calling out over the phone until Deanie finally said something.

"I'm okay," Deanie managed. "I think I was in shock for a sec."

"Well, hang on," Karen warned. "There's more news."

Deanie sat down on her bed, holding her head in her free hand, and listened.

"Dick wanted me to help lure Bill up to the Point tonight so Brian can beat him up. Dick made me call Bill at his uncle's and tell him that the Belles wanted to talk to him about the California job."

Deanie's head reeled. "How did Dick know about the California job?"

"Oh, I was stupid and let it slip about Bill's letter to Linda."

"Have you told the other Belles about this?"

"No," Karen was quick to answer. "I didn't see why I had to involve them."

Deanie began to fret. "I need to be up there, Karen."

"No, Deanie. We should stay far away from there."

"I have to, Karen. I can't let Bill tell Brian about the things I've done. I have this terrible feeling Brian will somehow beat it out of him."

"But there's nothing you can do to stop what these guys do, Deanie."

"I can at least be there to try, Karen. Maybe plead with Bill—something, anything."

"Do you feel well enough to be out in the cold wind?"

"I'll just stay in the car. I'm sure I'll be all right."

Karen finally relented. "I'll take you up there, but only if you promise to dress warmly."

Chapter Thirty-two

Brian's eyes watered from the wind as he took aim at a beer can lodged between the river rocks below him. Laying prone at the crest of the Point, with his head extended just over the cliff's edge, he squeezed the trigger of his .22 rifle. The constant roar of the river muffled most of the report, but the can leaped skyward, soaring out over the water before falling into the swift current. To the west, the sky looked like a painting, colored in soft layers of orange and red.

Brian felt anxious. He knew the action wasn't going to begin until after dark, but waiting at home made him even more nervous. He'd rehearsed, in his mind, all the scenarios he could imagine when he confronted Bill Slater. He felt he was prepared—prepared to give Bill Slater what he deserved. He didn't know how Dick was to accomplish it, but he hoped Slater would come.

Brian continued to shoot at cans and cottonwood limbs until the fading sunlight made it difficult to see. On that side of the Point, the wind and river made it impossible to hear a vehicle approach up the steep grade to Harvat's Flat. Brian didn't become aware of the pickup until it stopped behind his Chevy. It was Dick, in his dad's pickup. Dick got out quickly and limped over to Brian.

"What's the rifle for?" Dick asked. "I know you'd like to, but you can't kill the bastard."

Brian smiled. He walked over to his car and laid the rifle and box of shells in the front seat. "I remembered I had left it in the car. Thought I'd do something to take my mind off the wait."

"Buckley will be coming but won't show himself until after Slater gets here," Dick informed him.

"Why in the hell did you invite Buckley up here anyway? I can handle Slater."

"I know that. But after he gets his ass kicked, I want him to get tossed in jail. Remember that beer heist Sheriff McCarthy was trying to pin on you?

Brian was puzzled.

"Buckley wants to plant the other keg in Slater's trunk. When we tip off the sheriff, Slater gets busted and you and Buckley are finally off the hook."

"What makes you think that McCarthy is still interested in that beer heist? It's been several months now, and he hasn't nabbed anyone yet."

"Buckley says the thefts are still going on. Beer trucks are getting broken into on a regular basis. Buckley swears he isn't doing it anymore. I think McCarthy is waiting to catch these guys in the act and take them all in one big swoop."

"So you think I'm still on his suspect list?"

"Probably, but I wouldn't sweat it. Buckley sure is nervous about it, though. He's trying to steer the sheriff away from him any way he can. So why not lay it all on this good-for-nothing, Slater? I've got another surprise for the asshole, too."

"What kind of surprise?"

Dick grinned. "You'll see."

"So how did you manage to get Slater to come up here?"

"With the best lure in the universe, old buddy," Dick said, still grinning. "Pussy."

Dick re-parked his pickup so the headlights would shine back across the Point and asked Brian to do the same with his car. The night air was getting cooler. Brian and Dick snapped up their letterman jackets and leaned back against Brian's car to wait.

<h1 style="text-align:center">Chapter Thirty-three</h1>

It was dark when Karen drove up in her mother's Buick. Dressed in her maternity slacks and an extra-large sweatshirt, Deanie grabbed her jacket and hurried out into the night air. She welcomed the warmth inside the Buick. While she had waited for Karen, she fretted so much about the fight that she found the phone number of Bill's uncle and called, hoping Bill might be there and she could plead with him not to tell. When there was no answer, she became more frightened than ever.

"I just don't see how going up there is going to help, Deanie," Karen said, backing the car up. "If Bill's the bastard I think he is, he'll tell Brian whether Brian beats him up or not."

"I just have to do everything I can to stop him, Karen."

Karen got the car turned around and headed for the highway. She crossed the bridge over the Yellowstone. In the headlights, small pieces of debris blew across the road and gathered in the short new grass along the edge. Traffic was light, but from the car side mirror, Deanie noticed the glare of headlights some distance behind them. Karen noticed them too, as Deanie watched her glance repeatedly in the rearview mirror.

"I'll bet that's Bill back there," Karen said.

Deanie turned to look. "I can't tell what kind of car it is. It'd be like him to follow us."

"Want me to stop and wait for him? Dick would be pissed at me, but maybe you could talk to him right now."

"We can try," Deanie said.

Karen stopped along the highway, but when they looked back, the mystery car also stopped.

"It's him, all right," Karen said. "He's just playing games. Guess we should just keep going. He's expecting all the Belles up on the Point."

The gravel road was covered with potholes, and the Buick's shock absorbers offered little help with the bumps. The moon was still hidden behind the mountains, but the sky was clear and ablaze with stars. The radio was playing softly.

Suddenly, Deanie burst into tears, covering her face in her hands. "Oh, Karen," she cried. "I'm not handling this all very well. I know I'm being selfish, but I'm so afraid and I don't know what to do."

Karen reached across the seat and patted Deanie's arm. "I know you're afraid, Deanie. You have every right to be. You're my best friend, and I want to help, but I have to tell you that you are not being fair to either of these guys. Neither of them knows what you know. Whom I feel most sorry for is Brian. He's so blindly in love with you. He's been hurt, and I'm worried he's going to be hurt a lot more."

Deanie looked up, sniffling. "That's why I have to plead with Bill not to tell."

"But is it fair, Deanie? Should you continue to withhold the truth from Brian?"

"God, Karen. If I told Brian, I wouldn't have anyone."

Karen drove the Buick up the steep slope and onto Harvat's Flat. In the headlights, she spotted Brian and Dick down at the corner of the Point. They were both smoking a cigarette. As soon as Karen stopped the car next to Brian's Chevy, Deanie flew open her door and ran out to Brian, throwing her arms around him. Dick flicked away his cigarette and stepped inside Karen's car, allowing Brian and Deanie to be alone.

"You shouldn't be here, Deanie," Brian said.

Deanie clung to Brian. "I don't want you to fight, Brian. Please, let's go home."

Brian shook his head. "I can't," he said. "This is something I have to do—something I want to do."

Both of them kept glancing up to see if there were any lights approaching. The night air made Deanie shiver, and she motioned for Brian to sit with her in his car. Brian opened the driver's door and Deanie slipped in across the seat cushions, yelping when she bumped up against the .22 rifle.

The rifle startled her. "What are you doing with the gun?" she asked.

Brian lifted the rifle and shells over the seat and laid them in the back. "Now, don't be getting paranoid," he said. "I was just target practicing."

Suddenly, Deanie remembered the pistol she once saw in Bill's jockey box. Now she became worried that the confrontation might turn out to be more than just a fistfight.

Chapter Thirty-four

Although Brian didn't want Deanie there, he assumed she was there as part of the ruse Dick was using to lure Slater to the Point. While they waited, Dick told Brian about the letter to Linda and the dirty pictures. So it was true: Slater was a pimp, a recruiter of young pretty girls like the Belles. It was all the more reason to beat the crap out of him.

It seemed hours before a car finally came. When it did, it zoomed quickly out onto the flats. There was no doubt it was the red Pontiac. Brian's breathing increased, and he felt an ache deep in his stomach. Deanie tried her best to hold him back, but he stepped out into the headlights of the approaching car.

Dick called out to him from inside Karen's car, "I got your back, buddy!"

As soon as the headlights flashed across Brian, the Pontiac stopped abruptly, skidding slightly in the moist ground. The engine revved and the glass-pack mufflers rumbled. It was apparent that Slater was figuring things out and that perhaps this wasn't going to be a meeting with the Belles after all. Then suddenly, the Pontiac leaped forward and confidently came to a stop again, just inches from Brian's feet. Brian stood looking into the driver's window, both hands clinched, waiting for Slater to roll the window down. He could see Slater sitting inside, smoking. Brian tapped on the window, thinking he would pop Slater in the face as soon as the window came down. But the window remained closed, and Brian worried that Slater might panic and zoom away.

Then, out of the corner of his eye, Brian noticed Buckley's pickup slowly inching up behind the Pontiac with its lights off, almost touching the Pontiac's bumper. Brian wasn't sure Slater was aware the pickup was there. Whether he knew or not, Slater was trapped. He had nowhere to go, since ahead was the cliff's edge, leading to the rocks below. Brian wondered how Buckley was going to pull off the frame job. Slater wasn't simply going to allow someone to open up his trunk and toss a beer keg inside.

Suddenly, the door burst open, slamming sharply into Brian's knees, causing him to lose his balance. Brian stumbled and fell on his back. Before he knew it, Slater was on top of him, swinging his arms wildly, landing several punches to Brian's head and face. The Pontiac's interior light lit up a small area around him, and Brian could see the frightened, angry face of Bill Slater.

With adrenalin surging through him, Brian made two quick rolls to the side and managed to get to his feet. Slater charged, but as soon as he came in close, Brian delivered a sharp, crushing blow to Slater's nose.

All at once, the whole Point lit up as Deanie and Dick had flashed on the headlights. Brian lowered his head and shoulders and lunged, smacking Slater in the midsection. Driving hard with his legs, Brian picked Slater off his feet and slammed him flat on his back. Brian scrambled to get himself straddled across Slater's chest. When he had him pinned, he was able to throw blow after blow to Slater's face. Soon, Slater was covered in blood and he didn't struggle as much as he had. Still, Brian continued to pound on him.

"You son-of-a-bitch!" Brian yelled as he grabbed Slater by his throat. "You raped Deanie!"

Slater managed to look up at Brian, squinting through blood-splattered eyes. "Kiss my ass!" he shouted, spitting blood.

Brian continued to smack Slater's face, using the full weight of his shoulder. "I could kill you, Slater. You took something that wasn't yours."

Slater fell unconscious, but Brian continued to hit him until someone grabbed his arms from behind. It was Buckley.

"Hold on, West," Buckley said. "I think he's had enough." He pulled Brian a few feet away and then went back to attend to Slater. "Well, he isn't dead, but he's close to it!" he called back.

Dick came over quickly to help Brian to his feet. "Good job, buddy. You kicked his ass."

Buckley dragged Slater over to the Pontiac and propped him up against the front bumper. One part of Brian was glad Buckley was there to pull him off, but another part still wanted Slater dead. Still frustrated, he walked back to his car. Karen was in the front seat with Deanie, trying to calm her down. When Brian slid inside, Deanie threw her arms around him.

"Oh, God," she said, crying.

"It's over for now," Brian said.

He looked back at the Pontiac and watched Buckley and Dick load the keg of beer into the trunk of Slater's car. Then surprisingly, Brian noticed that Slater was beginning to move. Slater had managed to get back on his feet and stumbled toward the open door of the Pontiac. Neither Buckley nor Dick saw him. Brian leaped from the car and ran toward the Pontiac, but before he could get there, Slater stood upright in the open door, blood dripping from his chin, pointing a pearl-handled revolver at him. Abruptly, Brian saw a quick flash of gunpowder. There was a burning sensation in his left forearm. Stunned, he fell back onto the hard ground. When he looked up, Bill Slater was standing above him, pointing the revolver directly in his face.

Brian didn't move. He wasn't sure if Slater would shoot again.

"You're a dumb bastard, West," Slater said, wiping his eyes with his free hand. "I'm going to blow your fucking head off. Before I do, I want to set the record straight about Deanie. Yes, I fucked her, several times—and it wasn't rape, either. She was as eager as I was."

Brian could feel a sharp pain in his arm and a flow of blood, yet the words Slater spoke were much more painful. Suddenly, another shot sliced through the night air. This one much crisper, more powerful, whizzing just inches above Brian's head. A bullet slammed into Slater's chest with the thud of a well-thrown fastball. A girl screamed as Slater collapsed back against the Pontiac, the revolver dropping at his feet. Brian spun around to look behind him. In the dim light he saw Deanie standing off to the side of the Chevy, holding his .22 rifle and struggling with the bolt-action lever, apparently trying to get off another round. Buckley and Dick were hunkered down behind the Pontiac. Brian scrambled to his feet. Applying pressure to his arm, he raced back to the Chevy, keeping his head down in case Deanie managed to get off another round. When he reached her, she was in a panic, trembling, cursing the rifle and resisting Brian from taking it.

"He was going to kill you, Brian!" Deanie cried.

Brian looked through the window of his Chevy and saw Karen curled up on the floorboard. "Take Deanie home!" he hollered in at her.

Looking terrified, Karen stepped out of the car and hurried over to Deanie. She placed her arm around Deanie's shoulder and walked with her over to the Buick.

"Buckley thinks we'd better get Slater into the emergency room," Dick said excitedly when he got to the Chevy. "He's hit in the chest, wheezing and losing blood. What about you?"

"I'd better go in, too," Brian said. He took off his t-shirt and Dick helped to tie a tourniquet on the wound with it. "The bullet must have missed the bone, but it's starting to smart pretty good."

"This turned out kind of messy, Brian," Dick said, shaking nervously.

Brian nodded. He had a sick feeling in his stomach. "What are we going to do with Slater's Pontiac?"

"Let's leave it right where it is," Dick said. "Let the sheriff come and get it."

Buckley was the first to leave. Slater was conscious and slouched against the passenger door of the pickup, his face caked with blood and his dark hair all in a mess. Buckley had stuffed his own t-shirt under Slater's white shirt to help stop the bleeding.

When Karen headed out, she stopped momentarily in front of Brian. "I'm kind of worried about Deanie," she said from the window. "She's hysterical and can't stop shaking."

"Get her out of here, Karen," Brian said. "Just hurry and get her home."

"Can you drive with your arm like that?" Dick asked.

"I think so. I'll go in to the hospital. What are we going to do about all this, Dick?"

"I don't know, but we could be in a load of trouble. I might as well call the sheriff when I get to town. The hospital will alert him, anyway."

Brian slid into his car and waited for Dick to pull out in his pickup. The Pontiac's front door was still open with the interior light shining. Brian had decided to leave it that way, but when his Chevy's headlights flashed across Slater's pearl-handled revolver, he stopped to retrieve it. Dick's taillights were just starting down the steep grade. The Pontiac had an eerie silence about it, unoccupied, seemingly abandoned, its bright red finish glistening in the Chevy's headlights.

Brian reached down for the revolver and peered inside the Pontiac. The interior looked neat and clean but smelled of beer and cigarettes. For a moment he dwelled on an image of Deanie stretched out there on the front seat, naked. Again, he felt the raw, burning rage. Slater was beaten and barely alive, yet Brian's torment had not lessened. Perhaps it never would.

He tossed the revolver on the front seat and slammed the door shut. Just before getting back into his Chevy, he paused. He stepped back and reopened the Pontiac's door, reaching for the shift lever. Let the wind do the rest, he thought, throwing the Pontiac into neutral.

With the Pontiac pointed westward, Brian envisioned the wind gusts rocking it, causing it to start rolling, slowly toward the cliff's edge. As he drove down the Harvat's Flat grade, he savored the image of it falling silently through the blackened night air, its backend eventually overtaking its frontend, and crashing on its top against the jagged rocks along the river.

<h1 style="text-align:center">Chapter Thirty-five</h1>

Deanie's baby was born on July 15, 1961. It was a healthy boy, weighing in at seven pounds, six ounces. Deanie fell hopelessly in love, devoting every moment to him. She named him Brian Dean. Her parents were very supportive, helping to make her bedroom into a little home for her and the baby. Her father built a crib, and her mother painted it blue. Karen never stopped being Deanie's best friend, coming by most days after work to help with the baby.

The months leading up to the birth of Brian Dean were all a blur. Deanie remembered receiving her high school diploma in May, when Karen and the Belles brought it to her on graduation day. They were all dressed up and beaming with delight over finally getting out of school. Sherry won the ten-dollar prize for being the closest in picking the date Deanie would have the baby. Linda was quick to remind everyone that she had won the penis contest.

Most of the Belles had plans as to what they were going to do. Colleen and Sherry were going on to business school in Billings. Karen and Rita were staying in Livingston. Only Linda wanted to leave the state.

"I'm headed for California," she said confidently. "I'm going to enroll at UCLA, one way or another."

"Well, it might be another way," Karen said, rolling her eyes and grinning. "You're still dreaming about those nasty pictures Bill Slater sent you."

Bill Slater had died on the operating table at Livingston Memorial Hospital. Deanie remembered the many visits from Sheriff McCarthy, asking about every aspect of the shootings up on Harvat's Flat. When she kept insisting that she couldn't recall shooting the rifle, Sheriff McCarthy finally decided against filing any charges. He and the District Attorney felt it would be considered justifiable homicide, anyway.

Deanie remembered anguishing over Brian. She knew that the things Bill told him had shattered him, and she accepted the fact he'd never forgive her. She had hurt him—a hurt she feared might even destroy him. When Brian came to the hospital the day Brian Dean was born, he smiled and kissed her as she lay in bed nursing the baby. Frightened, she searched Brian's eyes for any reaction. As she removed the blanket from around Brian Dean's head, exposing his dark curly hair, she caught sight of a subtle wince just below Brian's eyes. Brian tried his best to conceal it, but Deanie knew he was devastated. At that moment, she knew she had lost him. When Brian left the hospital, she felt as though she had shot him through the heart with his .22 rifle.

On the morning of September 18, 1961, three days after his eighteenth birthday, Brian stepped up to the door of the westbound Greyhound bus, carrying a small brown leather suitcase his mother found for him. He also carried a dreadful sense of loss and homesickness. The bus would take him to Butte to be sworn in. From there, he'd fly to San Francisco and then take a bus into Fort Ord.

The day before was his last day at the station, and Orlen had wished him the best of luck. Only his mother and Dick came to the bus stop to see him off. His mother was with her boyfriend, Jerry. He wore a western shirt with pearl buttons and Tony Lama boots. His mother wore a pink dress that the wind ruffled up at her knees. She paced nervously as Brian readied himself to board. She brushed his hair with her hand and kissed him lightly on his cheek.

"I don't want you to leave, honey," she said, hugging him. "But I know there really isn't much for you here. Maybe the Army will give you a future."

Dick had a sad face. He shook Brian's hand and then softly punched him on the shoulder. "We were supposed to do this together," he said. "You know, the 'buddy plan' and all that."

Brian managed a smile. "I know. Wish we could have."

"I still don't think I'm 4F. My leg would have been just fine."

When the bus driver motioned for Brian to get aboard, Brian conjured up as much courage as he could and placed his foot on the first step.

"See you all in three years," he said, waving.

"Aren't you coming back on leave sometime?" Dick asked.

"I don't think so," Brian answered, not sure how truthful he was.

Only after he found a seat in the back of the bus and placed his suitcase under his seat did he allow himself to cry. His last year of high school had been a whirlwind, with Deanie at its heart. How he would ever get over her, he had no idea, but he had to try. The misery she dealt him hurt whether he was with her or not. He thought about the fight with Bill Slater and the events that followed. The Livingston Enterprise had reported everything, including the smashup of Slater's car on the rocks below the Point and the contents of its trunk: one stolen beer keg and a pair of shoes, matching the prints that were photographed at the scene of the Standard Oil station robbery. It was reported that Sheriff McCarthy finally closed the books on those two unsolved crimes. The Enterprise speculated that the winds up on Harvat's Flat blew the Pontiac right over the cliff's ledge. Brian's forearm had healed from the bullet wound. The bullet had lodged next to the bone but hadn't shattered anything. He passed the Army's physical easily.

From his window, Brian watched a Northern Pacific freight train struggling to make the grade over the Bozeman hill, with one engine pulling and two pushing. The grass was still green from the summer rains but would soon turn brown by the sun. Through the windshield, he watched the gray highway disappear beneath the bus, taking him farther and farther away from Livingston. He was more frightened than he had ever been. Suddenly, he panicked as beads of sweat trickled down the side of his head, onto his neck. He was breathing so hard, he could hardly catch his breath. He wasn't sure he could go through with it. For a moment, he felt compelled to run up the aisle of the bus, screaming for the driver to let him off.

The white lines of the highway reminded him of yard-markers, bringing to mind something Coach LeClaire had said the night of the last football game. "There's nobody else who can do this, West. You'll just have to play hurt."

When the bus reached Bozeman and passed by the Hawks' football field, Brian remembered the sight of the beer spewing from the ruptured keg and all the fire and smoke on the field. He couldn't help but smile. He pushed back in the bus seat. Behind him was the only world he ever knew. What lay ahead, he couldn't even imagine. He wished Dick were there.

9 7 9 8 8 9 3 3 0 2 6 5 3